SEASONS REMEMBERED

A TIME TO EMBRACE

Linda Shands

INTERVARSITY PRESS
DOWNERS GROVE, ILLINOIS 60515

InterVarsity Press® is the book-publishing division of InterVarsity Christian Fellowship®, a student movement active on campus at hundreds of universities, colleges and schools of nursing in the United States of America, and a member movement of the International Fellowship of Evangelical Students. For information about local and regional activities, write Public Relations Dept., InterVarsity Christian Fellowship, 6400 Schroeder Rd., P.O. Box 7895, Madison, WI 53707-7895.

Cover illustration: David Darrow
ISBN 0-8308-1932-0

Printed in the United States of America ∞

Library of Congress Cataloging-in-Publication Data

Shands, Linda, 1944-
    A time to embrace/Linda Shands.
      p.   cm.—(Seasons remembered)
    ISBN 0-8308-1932-0
    1. World War, 1939-1945—United States—Fiction. 2. Married
people—United States—Fiction. I. Title. II. Series: Shands,
Linda, 1944- Seasons remembered.
    PS3569.H329T555   1994
    813'.54—dc20   94-43030
                                            CIP

17	16	15	14	13	12	11	10	9	8	7	6	5	4	3	2	1
09	08	07	06	05	04	03	02	01	00	99	98	97	96	95		

Thank you:
Elsie, Linda, Melody, Heather,
Janice, Tanya and Michelle,
for encouragement and critique;
Kristen and Bobbie,
for coming to the rescue;
and Mama,
for a treasury of memories.

Prologue

When Libby turned fourteen we celebrated her birthday like we always did: with Aunt Rose's enchiladas, vanilla ice cream, and Mama's recipe for chocolate cake. I could never make it taste as light and rich as hers, but no one seemed to notice. They ate up every scrap.

After dinner the men gathered around the television set to watch a ball game. I never understood how they could remember the score of every Yankees game since 1945, but they did and spent hours arguing over who hit this home run and who held the record for the most RBIs.

While they lounged around the living room I got out the photo albums, and we girls sat at the kitchen table looking at pictures and remembering the old days, as Libby called them.

We thumbed through Libby's baby pictures and came to one with her in a sailor dress sitting on her daddy's shoulders big as you please, holding a red balloon on a cardboard stick and grinning into the camera with her father's smile.

Libby still has her father's smile, and expressive eyes. They're blue, like mine, but quick to dance with laughter, or spark fire when she's mad. She's strong, our Libby, strong and smart. Even at fourteen she scares me some, with her zest for life and her incessant curiosity.

Libby loved to look at photo albums. Her eyes glowed as she asked about the day we took that picture, and I explained, like I did every year, how we'd gone to pick up her father on his last day in the Navy and stopped by the park to celebrate. Her daddy bought her a red balloon, then picked her up and put her on his shoulders for a ride back to the car. That was 1946. She was two years old and her father's pride and joy.

We'd finished that album and I started to put it away when Libby spoke up. "Get the other one, Mom. The one from when you were young."

I looked at Aunt Rose. Her face had that quiet, settled look from years of trials that had transformed anxiety into peace. Her hair had turned a soft blue-gray. She wore it short and curly now with a home-done perm.

"Of course we must look at that one too," she nodded when I hesitated. "Get them all down, Cissy. I haven't seen them in years."

I hadn't looked at them in ages either. Truth to tell, I didn't want to look at them now. "Old ghosts are best laid to rest," I heard Grandma Eva say just like she was standing in the room. But I didn't want to disappoint Aunt Rose, and it was Libby's birthday, so I fetched the albums.

We started with the oldest first. There were snaps of me with my sister Krista, who died when I was eleven, and some of my brother Chuckie that Papa had taken before the baby, Grace, was born. Mama had managed to save the pictures even when they moved her to the state hospital.

Mama died when Libby was three, but there were pictures of her too, taken on the few occasions she had come home to visit.

She never stayed long though. "I'm not comfortable in the outside world anymore, Celia," she'd say. "I have my home here at the sanatorium and I've no reason to leave it. Anyway, I don't want to be a burden to you or Rose." Then she'd have one of her spells that convinced us she truly was better off under a doctor's care.

Libby knew all about my early years—Mama's illness, my time at the orphanage, how Chuckie and Grace had been adopted and how I had found a home with Uncle Edward and Aunt Rose. They had made it clear from the start how much they loved me. Even Billy and Mary Margaret treated me like a sister instead of just a cousin.

We'd told Libby about Papa when she was twelve. Some of it, anyway. She knew he'd gone to prison for embezzling money and she knew he'd died. We still hadn't told her how.

The last page of that album held a picture of him taken just after Chuckie was born. He was standing by the porch next to Mama's pink camellia bush posing for the camera in a starched white shirt, dark blue jacket and blue striped tie. The knot was slightly crooked, tucked just right of center under his collar.

"Looks like you're ready for a hanging, Charles," Mama had said when the film was done.

"Isn't that the same picture you keep on your dresser?" Libby asked.

I nodded. I had just turned fourteen, Libby's age, when Papa was executed for a crime he hadn't committed. Two days later, I packed away my diary and a few other childhood mementos in a brown paper box Uncle Edward brought home from the Nabisco factory.

But I kept Papa's picture out, on my side of the dresser where I could look at it every day and remember. He was dead because Roy Cummings lied, and I wanted Roy and all his cronies to pay. Like Mama said, Papa may have done some things to be ashamed of, but he was not a murderer. Back then, I had only wanted to see his name cleared and the real murderers dead. Later, I had a copy of the picture made for the album and kept the original in its frame, to remind me that God restores everything for good, in his own time.

I looked at Libby, eyes sparkling, her cheeks wrinkled with laughter. *Was I ever that young?* I wondered.

Libby handed the last album to her great-aunt Rose and threw her arms around my neck. "Thanks, Mom," she whispered. "It's been the best birthday ever."

A horn honked outside.

"Rachel's here!" Libby squealed. "And Aunt Dotty. I wonder what they brought me."

I shook my head as she ran from the kitchen. "Have we spoiled her, Aunt Rose? Was I that excitable when I was in high school?"

I thought I saw a tear gleam in the corner of her eye, but her cheeks were bright and she was smiling. "My land, no! You never had the time, and we never had the means to spoil you."

She was right. Things were different in 1936. We'd survived the Great Depression better than some, but another monster lurked just around the corner, ready to pounce and gobble us up, like a lion with its prey.

Chapter
One

For the most part, my high-school years were like the eye of a hurricane after all that had gone on before and what would happen later. Still, I'm not sure I'd want to do it all again.

I remember Grandma Eva saying once, "I'm glad the good Lord doesn't allow us to see the future. We'd be so busy fretting about what's to come we couldn't enjoy the here and now."

I admit I would never have survived the first few days at Central High if it hadn't been for Mary Margaret. She was already a junior and in the Girl's League. It was their job to show us "scrubs" the ropes, and Mary Margaret offered to take me under her wing.

The sun was roasting acorns on the sidewalks as we walked the mile from home to school. The bus would only pick up kids as far away as Front Street, and we lived two blocks this side on Sherwood Lane.

I liked to walk. It gave me time to think. I loved to feel the sun warm my hair and listen to the robins serenade the morning. But my first day of high school I hardly noticed anything except flutters of excitement mixed with fear that made my stomach churn and my knees feel like Jell-O.

By the time we made it to the administration office, Mary

Margaret had to grab my arm to keep me from running back home.

"Don't be a ninny, Cissy. No one's going to bother you with me around."

Bother me? I hadn't even thought of that. It was just that the school was so big. I had visions of getting lost in the halls and being late to class or, worse, missing class altogether and getting in trouble my first day. I had heard stories of upper-classmen playing pranks on the younger students, but it never dawned on me that someone might play a trick on me until Mary Margaret said it.

My stomach lurched again. *Grow up, you idiot,* I told myself. *You're fourteen, not a baby anymore.*

Mary Margaret handed me a piece of paper with a list of classes in one column and room numbers in another. "See, this is your schedule. I've been excused from my own classes to show you around," she hissed in my ear, "so don't be a baby and embarrass me."

I happened to know that juniors and seniors didn't have classes that day, but I kept quiet. I didn't want her to get in a huff and leave me on my own.

A week later, I could find my classes fine. I did have one nightmare though. I was scared to death I'd forget my locker combination and my locker partner would already be in class and I wouldn't be able to get my books without going to the office. Then I'd be marked tardy and get a demerit for being in the halls without a pass.

I finally got the nerve to tell my friend Dotty how I felt.

"I know," Dotty nodded. "I have trouble remembering my combination too. Look." She pulled back the sleeve of her blouse and showed me a set of numbers she'd printed on the back of her wrist in blue ink. "My brother says this always works."

Dotty's brother was pretty smart. He used to be fun too, but when Mr. Johnson died and Mrs. Johnson moved to San Bernardino to live with Dotty's grandma, he went quiet and moody. He had to start his senior year at a new high school, and he didn't like that one bit. I guess all the changes were harder on him than on Dotty. At least she had me around again.

The next morning I made the mistake of wearing my blue print blouse with the short sleeves. Aunt Rose saw the numbers on my wrist and stopped me as I was going out the door.

"That looks awful, Cissy. Why don't you just look up the combination in your notebook until you have it memorized?"

I didn't want to sass, but I didn't want to wash the numbers off either.

"How can I look it up if the notebook's in my locker?"

She stared at me, then coughed like she had a tickle in her throat and shooed me out the door.

* * *

As it turned out, Mary Margaret did have to save me from a prank. It wasn't meant for me, but I got caught in it just the same.

Samuel Levi, my locker partner, was a freshman too. He was cute, except he wore glasses and had some pimples on his chin. We had social studies together second period and usually got to our locker at the same time.

On the third Tuesday after school started, I was in a hurry because I'd walked Dotty to her history class. I wasn't dumb enough to run in the halls, but I could walk pretty fast, and I was huffing and puffing by the time I got upstairs to the locker hall. Sam stood there fooling with the lock, but it wouldn't open.

I moved in front of him. "Here, let me do it or we'll both be late."

I read the numbers off my wrist three times, but the lock wouldn't open for me either.

Sam was sweating. He wiped his glasses on his shirt. We both knew the bell would ring in two more minutes. Our class was three halls away.

Before I could panic, Mary Margaret came around the corner hand in hand with Wesley Harris. She let him loose when she saw me. "What's going on?" She left Wesley standing in the middle of the hall and came over. "You two better get going, the bell's about to ring."

"We can't get it open," I gasped. My worst fears were about to come true. I'd be late for class and caught in the hall with a boy, to boot.

Mary Margaret looked at the lock, then backed away and read the numbers at the top of the metal door. "That's not your locker, you ninnies," she laughed. "Yours is number sixteen, right here." She pointed to another door two lockers down.

I looked daggers at Sam. He started to argue, "It *is* our locker. See this white mark? I put it on the door so I could find it right away."

"Why don't you just read the number?" I growled and spun the dial on our real locker. I grabbed my books and made it to class one second before the bell. Sam was a little slower and Mr. Sours marked him tardy.

I felt sorry for him. At lunch we examined the locker and found where his white mark had been rubbed out and repainted on the other one. Someone had scratched the letters *JEW* over the rubbed-out mark. They were so faint you could hardly see them and I told him to never mind. Uncle Edward says people who do things like that have mean spirits and will be sorry in the end.

Sam didn't want to talk about it then. Any of it. But when I knew him better, he explained that he sometimes saw numbers backwards and the only way he could be sure he had the right locker was to mark it with white ink he'd borrowed from the art room. After that day though, he never got the doors mixed up again.

* * *

"It's rumored that this fellow Hitler has taken over Austria." Uncle Edward turned the page on his morning paper and took a sip of coffee from the pottery mug Billy had made him for his birthday. He made a face and flicked a scrap of paint from the handle. "Do something with this, will you, Rose?" He handed her the cup and went back to his paper.

She rinsed the cup and set it on the sink. "That new *Life* magazine had his picture. They say he's crazy. Do you think he could be a threat to America, Edward?"

"Don't be silly, Rose. Still, I feel sorry for those poor people over there." He turned his head in my direction. "Look here, Cissy, it says that new outfielder for the Yankees, Joe DiMaggio, hit another home run. Mark my words, he's one to keep an eye on."

I made a mental note to tell Billy about Joe DiMaggio. The stuff about Hitler didn't mean much to me. Germany and Italy were only places on the map in my geography book. Sam had relatives somewhere in Russia, but none of my other friends were too interested in what was going on in Europe. That is, until Edward VII, prince of Wales, renounced his throne to marry Mrs. Wallis Simpson. That event set our world back on it its heels.

Billy's fifth-grade teacher was English, and she almost went into shock. "The ideah!" Billy mimicked in a perfect British accent. "The future king of England forgetting his station to marry an American. And a divorcée. How utterly appalling!"

"William, mind your manners," Aunt Rose scolded.

"Have some respect, young man," Uncle Edward said, turning his head and smiling.

Mary Margaret flounced her skirt and stuck her nose in the

air. "What a wicked woman she must be," she whispered when the others left the room, "to divorce one man and seduce a prince."

"He'll be king someday," I reminded her.

"Can you imagine?" She tried to look indignant, but I could see the spark in her eyes. "When I marry," she crooned, "it will be true love. I'd never get divorced, not even for the king of England."

I could have reminded her of those words later.

Chapter Two

In November, the Girl's League sponsored an after-game dance. I hadn't planned to go to the dance, but everyone went to the football games, including Aunt Rose and Uncle Edward.

"Don't sit with Mama or Daddy," Mary Margaret whispered while we were fetching sweaters from the closet in the entryway. "Mama gets too excited and Daddy yells at the referees. Everyone looks at them. It's just too embarrassing!"

I started to ask, "Where should I sit then?" but she kept on talking while she primped in the mirror over the mantle.

"Are my sides even?" she asked without waiting for an answer. "I declare, I can't do anything with my hair these days. Wesley says he likes it, though. Maybe I'll cut it and put it up in pin curls like Mae West." She stuck her hand on her hip and glided around the room patting her hair. "Say, big boy," she purred, "why don't you come up and see me sometime?"

"Oh, Mary Margaret!"

Neither of us had seen Aunt Rose come in the room. I was too busy laughing at Mary Margaret's antics, and Mary Margaret was too engrossed in catching Wesley Harris to see anyone else at all.

Aunt Rose steadied Mary Margaret's shoulders and peered at

her face. "You don't need all that lipstick, young lady." She turned her toward the bathroom. "And wipe off some of that rouge. You're going to a football game."

Aunt Rose looked me over too. I was glad I hadn't put on any lipstick. Why should I? Jake wasn't here. He went to Franklin High in L.A. and it was too far to come for a silly football game. Anyway, Jake preferred baseball.

"You shouldn't expect Jake to come around as much, now that school's started," Uncle Edward had cautioned. "He has his own studies to attend to."

"He's right, dear," Aunt Rose added. "You've known Jake a long time. It won't hurt you to make other friends." I knew they were right, but I missed him just the same.

When we got to the field, Mary Margaret went straight to the center section reserved for upperclassmen and plopped herself down next to Wesley. Billy had brought a friend, and Uncle Edward made them sit in front of him.

I was about to sit down beside Aunt Rose in spite of Mary Margaret's warning, when Dotty grabbed my elbow and led me to the benches two rows down.

Halfway through the game, Sam squeezed between us and handed Dotty and me each a stick of Wrigley's.

"Whatya say we go to the dance, Cissy? I can pick you up at six. That'll give you time to change."

My chin dropped to my knees. I'd never thought of going to the dance at all, let alone with anyone but Jake.

I felt Dotty's finger in my ribs and realized I should quit staring and answer. The trouble was, I didn't know what to say.

"Uh, I don't know. I mean I don't think so. I don't know how to dance."

He smiled, "That's okay. I'm a good dancer, I'll teach you. See you after the game."

He wadded up the foil wrapper from his gum and tossed it

in the air. I caught it before it could hit the ground. Sam grinned at me again and strode off, big as you please, back to the group of boys he'd been sitting with.

"What'll you wear?" Dotty had to hold on to the bench to keep from jumping up and down.

"Why, my new blue dress," I said without thinking. It turned out to be a good choice.

The Sam that showed up at six was different from the one I shared my locker with. He had on a white shirt, brown slacks and a dark brown tie. His hair looked three shades darker and smelled like bay rum.

Why, he's handsome, I thought and felt a twinge of guilt.

Uncle Edward relaxed when he found out Sam's father was driving us. "You two have a good time." He smiled and shut the door.

Sam took my arm. "You look beautiful, Cissy. You'll be the prettiest girl there."

I felt my face heat up, but it was nice to have someone besides Uncle Edward tell me I was pretty.

*   *   *

Sam was right. He was a good dancer. A good teacher too.

Dean Fuller, president of the Boy's Federation, cranked up the Victrola and put on some Glenn Miller tunes. Sam was surprised when he saw I could already do the swing.

"I learned last year," I told him when I caught my breath. "I lived with a foster family who liked to dance."

Sam brought me a glass of punch. Then he taught me the two-step and the Lindy hop. We stayed until the dance ended at nine, and his father came and took me home.

"You look chipper," Uncle Edward said. "Did you have a good time?"

Aunt Rose laid down her book. "You should get some rest now, Cissy," she said before I could answer. She started to get up from the couch, but Uncle Edward put his hand on her arm.

I kissed them both good-night and went up to my room. Aunt Rose had been so nervous lately and I couldn't figure why. She'd been sharp with everyone and that was not her way.

When I got up at midnight to use the bathroom, they were both still on the couch and Mary Margaret still wasn't home.

* * *

On California winter nights you can almost touch the stars. I liked to pull on one of Uncle Edward's flannel shirts and sit on the front porch steps to watch the sky. I could pick out the Big and Little Dippers and a few other constellations, but for the most part I just admired their fire and talked to the one who made them.

Nighttime was my time to pray. Oh, I knew God heard me anytime I talked to him. But at night, in the dark, he seemed closer somehow, like a good friend when you're lonely and need someone to confide in.

I'd packed my diary away and I surely didn't want it back. It held too many memories that were best left in the past.

Dotty was a swell girl and fun to be with, but I couldn't confide my secrets to her—they'd be plastered in the *Panther Press* by morning. Mary Margaret was a whirl of flared skirts, red lipstick and fancy hairdos. She was busy with the Girl's League, her friends and, of course, Wesley Harris. Sam and I were fast becoming friends, but I couldn't tell my feelings to a boy. Not even Jake, because we hardly ever saw each other. Anyway, most of my secret thoughts were about him.

So only God knew how much I missed Jake and how I wanted him to kiss me again. I didn't pray that in so many words, but I did ask would he please keep Jake safe and let him come to see me again soon. If God knew my thoughts like Aunt Rose said he did, then he knew about the kissing part without me praying it.

Sam tried to kiss me. Right after Christmas break at the Backward Dance, where the girls had to ask the boys to go. Dotty even bought her date a carnation for his lapel.

Jake couldn't come, of course. He'd written me a letter in a Christmas card saying how he missed me and wished he could come visit. "Times are still hard around here," he wrote. "Ma keeps a garden, even in winter, and there's always chores to do.

"I'm not doing so good in school. Things are picking up at Gimble's Drug Store and I'm working more hours. Pa says I'm old enough to pay rent and I'd better stay off the freight cars or I'll wind up dead along some stretch of tracks. So, no money, no time, and no transportation. Some life, huh, babe?"

I spent some time being angry with Jake's pa and worried about Jake flunking out of school, but Aunt Rose convinced me it wouldn't do either Jake or me any good to fret over it.

"Life is full of disappointments, sweetheart. Just keep Jake in your prayers. Things will work out, you'll see."

Anyway, I wanted to go to the dance, so I asked Sam.

"Only if you wear your blue dress again," he teased.

We danced to almost every tune, even the slow ones. When they played "The Way You Look Tonight," I felt breathless and had to sit down. "I'm sorry, Sam. I guess I'm just tired."

I couldn't tell him I felt dizzy when he held me that way— so close I could smell his Old Spice and count the goosebumps on his neck above his collar.

"Let's walk awhile, maybe you'll feel better." He helped me up and led me through the gym out to the parking lot.

The cool air did feel good, but when he stopped and pulled me close again to kiss me, I knew I didn't want to. I wanted us to be good friends and nothing more.

"I can't," I said and turned my head away just as his father pulled into the parking lot.

Chapter
Three

In May of 1937 the Hindenburg dirigible blew up in New Jersey, Jake quit school, and Roy Cummings turned up dead.

We were listening to George Burns and Gracie Allen on the radio. Gracie was always looking for her brother. He'd been missing a long time, and I pictured myself, years from now when I was her age, still searching for Chuckie. George and Gracie made it all sound funny, but I never laughed at that part of the show.

The news reporter interrupted right in the middle of one of Gracie's stories with news about the airship. Uncle Edward put down his paper and turned the volume up.

"Thirty-six people. So many at once!" Aunt Rose shook her head. "How could anyone ever want to ride in one of those things? They're too dangerous!"

Uncle Edward looked thoughtful. "It is a shame, Rose, but sometimes the price of progress is high."

Mary Margaret said, "Oh dear, I'm late for my date with Wesley," and Billy asked Uncle Edward, "What's a dirigible?"

I felt cold all over.

That night I sat on the porch and thought how much I hated death. It was so final. For us here on earth anyway. Those people who died had families who would miss them. The way I missed Papa and Krista. Aunt Rose said we'd see them again someday. But what about those other families?

I tried to talk to Mama about it when I went to see her the end of May, but she just smiled and said, "When I get to heaven, I'll ask Papa for you."

Then she went away inside herself again, so I just kissed her cheek and let it be.

Aunt Rose said she thought Mama was getting better. "She has longer periods where she knows who we are and can carry on a conversation. I wish you could see her more often, Cissy. It would be so good for both of you."

But I was only allowed to visit once every six months until I turned sixteen.

"We're breaking the rules as it is," the hospital director had explained to Uncle Edward. "She's really not supposed to come at all."

I wanted to know who had made such a stupid rule, but of course I didn't ask. Anyway, as much as I missed Mama and wanted to see her, the hospital itself gave me the creeps. The high brick walls, stuffy lobby and dark, sour-smelling hallways made me want to run the other way. And everything was painted gray—prison gray, like the stationery Papa used for his last letter.

We had been to see Mama on Saturday evening, and Jake showed up Sunday after church.

Uncle Edward was cutting up the pot roast for our Sunday dinner when we heard the rattle of a truck pulling into the driveway.

"Who could that be?" Aunt Rose folded her napkin and counted the potatoes in the bowl. "I hope it's not the Hendersons, there's not nearly enough to go around."

I had to bite my lip to keep from laughing. We'd have to serve an entire cow to satisfy the Hendersons. There were only three of them, Mr. and Mrs. and their six-year-old Elroy, but they were all three shaped like bowling pins and could tuck away the food like there was no tomorrow.

Billy pulled his plate a little closer when the doorbell rang.

"I'll go." Uncle Edward put down the carving knife and disappeared into the living room. He was back in no time, grinning like a turkey gobbler the day after Thanksgiving.

"There's someone here to see you, Cissy," he said, giving Aunt Rose the strangest look.

"Who on earth . . . ?" Aunt Rose started to stand, but Uncle Edward touched her shoulder and she sat back down.

"Go see, Cissy," he prodded, "then you can both come in to dinner. Mary Margaret will set another plate."

Mary Margaret opened her mouth, then shut it again. As I stood up and peeked into the living room, I could already hear her opening the cupboard.

I couldn't believe my eyes. Jake stood by the fireplace, his arm draped over the back of the captain's chair, studying the pictures on the mantle like he'd never seen any of us before.

I must have made a noise, because he turned and looked at me, his face a puzzle of emotion. For a minute I thought something was wrong. But then he smiled and held out his arms. The next thing I knew he was about to break my ribs with the biggest bear hug I'd ever had.

My head was whirling. I wanted to laugh and cry at once, but I didn't do either. I could barely keep my feet under me till Jake pushed me back and held my shoulders.

"You look great, Cissy," he smiled. "I've missed you, you know."

"I missed you too, Jake," I stammered. I was glad I'd changed into my new gold jumpsuit with the short, cuffed sleeves and flared legs. My hair had darkened some and I'd let it grow. I'd fixed it just that morning, sides swept up and fastened with a comb, the back rolled under in a style Mary Margaret had convinced me to copy from her latest issue of *Vogue*. I still had a touch of lipstick on from church, and I knew I looked okay.

He just stood there staring until I felt my face go red and remembered my manners. I tried to say, "Come into the kitchen," but it came out as a squeak. I cleared my throat and tried again. "Aunt Rose has pot roast, and carrots and potatoes too. And homemade rolls."

Now Jake looked embarrassed. "Oh. I didn't mean to interrupt your dinner." He twisted his cap. "I had the afternoon free and I just thought . . . What I mean is, I just wanted to see you, Cissy. I have my father's truck and I thought maybe we could take a ride."

Aunt Rose saved the situation. "Jake!" She moved across the room and gave him a hug. "How nice to see you. You're just in time for dinner." She took his arm and led him toward the kitchen. "Now, I'll have no nonsense. You've come a long ways and you must have something to eat."

Jake talked politics with Uncle Edward, teased Mary Margaret about Wesley and entertained Billy with baseball stories. All the while, Aunt Rose passed the food bowls and kept his plate full until he pushed away the meat platter and declared surrender.

"You're a great cook, Mrs. Crandall, but I can't eat another bite. In fact I'm sure Ma won't have to feed me for a week."

Aunt Rose looked doubtful. Jake was still thin as a rail, though his shoulders had filled out some.

"It's a wonder that boy survives," I heard her tell Uncle Edward later. "All those children. I'm sure he goes without so there will be enough to go around."

Uncle Edward only chuckled. "I wouldn't bet on it, Rose. Kids his age burn off everything they eat. He'll fill out when he's older."

I wanted to say, "Jake's no kid, he's seventeen," but they didn't know I could hear them and it would have been rude to interrupt.

Uncle Edward let me go in the truck, but I could tell he didn't really want to. He took Jake aside before we left, and Jake wouldn't tell me what he said. "Man talk," was all Jake would say.

"Drive carefully," Uncle Edward said, holding the door, "and have her home by five. There's church this evening."

"Yes, sir." Jake tipped his hat and ground the engine.

The truck bench was hard, the leather cracked and peeling, showing stuffing underneath. There was a big hole on the passenger side, and Jake patted the seat closer to him. "Move this way, Cissy," he hollered over the rattle of the motor. We hit a bump and I bounced in that direction, so I stayed where the truck had put me.

We drove straight out of town toward the mountains. Sunlight splashed the streets with gold, and sparrows lined the telephone wires. Their music seemed to soften the clatter of the truck, and a warm breeze from Jake's open window ruffled my hair. I started to tuck the rolls back in, but Jake took my hand away.

"Let it be, Cissy. I like it when your hair blows free."

He kept my hand until he had to shift to go uphill. I never even thought to ask where we were going. It was enough to sit so close to Jake and have him hold my hand. I truly wished the ride would last forever.

We pulled onto a gravel road, and Jake put both hands on the wheel. I was disappointed at first until I saw the lake.

Jake stopped the truck at the top of a hill and cut the motor. Silence like a summer Sunday morning settled on the day. We could see the world from there. The best part anyway. Miles of green-blue water rimmed by pine trees, splashed against a rocky shore.

We sat there, still as statues, breathing in the cool air. The water rippled as a fish jumped, then smoothed out again, a flawless mirror on the forest floor. Another silver body broke the surface just as the harsh cry of an osprey shattered the silence. I gasped, both horrified and awed as the large bird claimed its even larger prey and flew off to the top of a tall silver pine, the quivering victim clutched tightly in its talons.

"Birds have to eat too," Jake said and put his arm around my shoulders. "That's the nature of things."

I wondered how he knew what I was thinking. A year ago Jake would have teased me for being squeamish and found something slimy to chase me with. But not today.

"I'm quitting school, Cissy." His voice was quiet, sad and wistful, like the dying of a happy dream. "Pa says I'm old enough to work full time and help him feed the family."

"Jake, you can't! Why, the school year is almost over and you only have one more year to go."

He shrugged and turned his head away.

I wondered what that would mean to us. Maybe we could see each other more. Maybe he could take me to the end-of-school dance. Sam would understand. My heart suddenly felt lighter and I started to ask, but Jake seemed far away, staring at the lake like it had the answers to a million questions.

"What will you do?" I asked instead.

His arm tightened around my shoulders, but he wouldn't look at me.

"Mr. Gimble says I can work for him. Behind the counter as a clerk. Says he'll train me to make sodas and fry up burgers and stuff."

I knew that wasn't what Jake wanted. He had better things to do in life, like graduate and be a pilot in an air machine. Not a dirigible. A fighter plane. One of the new ones the Navy was building. He'd talked of that the last time we had seen each other. "I want to be somebody, Cissy," he had said. "I want to do something grand with my life, something everyone will look up to and remember."

I felt a stirring of anger in my soul. How could his father make him give up such great ambitions? But I didn't want to talk bad to Jake about his pa. It would only make him feel worse. Instead I touched his cheek, like Aunt Rose touched Uncle Edward when she wanted him to look at her.

Jake looked. His dark eyes held such sadness, it made me want to cry.

"It's okay, Jake," I whispered. "Everything will be okay." I remembered him telling me that once, and I wished I could believe it.

He had me home in plenty of time for church, but he wouldn't go. "I have to get the truck back before Pa thinks I drove it in a ditch." He shook hands with Uncle Edward, punched Billy on the shoulder and kissed my cheek good-by.

That hurt my feelings. Last year he had kissed me on the lips and I was just thirteen! But then I remembered Aunt Rose and Uncle Edward standing on the porch and understood.

He was a gentleman, my Jake.

Chapter
Four

Two crabbers found Roy Cummings on a Sunday morning when the tide went out. He was stuffed in a fish barrel wedged between the pilings under the Santa Monica Pier. His throat was slit from ear to ear and he'd been dead at least a week.

Uncle Edward said it was bound to happen. "Look at the company he kept!"

Aunt Rose made our lives a misery for weeks. Watched us all like a hawk. She wouldn't let Mary Margaret or me go anywhere by ourselves, and Billy couldn't play with anyone she didn't know.

"Oh, Edward, what if those horrible men come around here?"

Uncle Edward hushed her when he saw Billy and me standing in the doorway. "They won't," he promised. "But nonetheless, you kids be careful and don't talk to strangers."

I remembered how upset Mama had been when Roy Cummings started coming around, and I realized it had to do with more than just their past.

I promised Uncle Edward I'd be careful. After all, I had seen Roy with another man and heard them admit their connection with Lou Berdowski's murderer. But I really wasn't afraid. Why would they come after me? Roy Cummings was the one who had framed my papa for the killing. He'd admitted it, and I'd heard that too. I didn't feel much of anything about him being dead—not sorry, not even glad he got what he deserved. I only thought how now we'd never know who really killed Lou Berdowski and never clear Papa's name.

But Jake reminded me that wasn't true. "There's the other one, Cissy," he said on his next Sunday visit to the house. "The man in the alley. You know, the one who gave me this scar." He rubbed his hand across the jagged white track above his right eye.

I reached out to smooth it with my finger. Jake's face bore a lot of scars. And a crooked nose, broke twice in fights. He was a scrapper but still handsome, I thought, in spite of the marks on his face. "They give him character," Mary Margaret said. And I agreed.

I just shrugged and handed him another plate to dry. "I didn't see him, Jake. Not his face, anyway. And he doesn't know us from Adam."

"He knows me," Jake insisted, "or he'd recognize me, at least. And he has no idea whether or not you saw his face." Jake put the last plate away and handed me the towel. "Just be careful, Cissy." He looked for all the world like Papa used to when he said good-by to Mama on a workday morning. Like she was a piece of china that might break while he was gone.

I nodded yes and realized there might be more to Roy Cummings's dying than met the eye.

Evidently the police thought so too.

A few days later, a tall man in a dark gray suit, white shirt and blue striped tie knocked on our door and asked to speak to Uncle Edward.

Aunt Rose sent Billy to the back yard to play and me and Mary Margaret to our room.

"Well, I never, " Mary Margaret huffed when she shut the

door behind us. "What could he possibly have to say that would interest me anyway?"

I knew she was miffed at being sent to her room "like a schoolgirl," she said. I wanted to point out that she *was* still a schoolgirl, but thought it best not to say it just then.

Mary Margaret was almost seventeen. She thought she was grown up and should be included in every adult conversation. Aunt Rose had to boss her even more often now than usual, which only made matters worse.

Aunt Rose was always tired lately. She'd started having migraine headaches around the same time Mary Margaret started dating Wesley Harris. They were horrible things that made her vomit and sent her to bed for hours at a time.

I had just talked Mary Margaret into loaning me her latest *Vogue* magazine, when Uncle Edward called me downstairs. Mary Margaret nearly had a hissy when Aunt Rose said, "Not you, young lady. Don't you have your studies to tend to?"

Uncle Edward sat me next to him on the sofa. "Cissy, this is Sergeant Harman. He's a detective with the Los Angeles County Police. He'd like to ask you some questions."

The detective was not a gentle man in speech or manner, and after two minutes I knew he meant business.

"What else did you notice about the other man?" he asked after I told him again what Jake and I had heard in the alley the day Papa died.

"Nothing," I stammered. "I mean he was big and wore black polished shoes and a blue striped suit."

"That could be anyone, Miss Summers," the man pressed. "Can't you remember anything else about him? Was he bald? Did he have a mustache or a scar?"

I shook my head. I'd been too upset that day to notice what that other man had looked like. I'd only focused on Roy Cummings and the things he said. Like: "Today's the day," and

"Summers don't know nothing anyway."

Uncle Edward put his arm around my shoulder, and I looked at him gratefully. I felt cold and shaky and wanted this whole thing to be over. Maybe finding out the real killer didn't matter. It was too late to help Papa, and I didn't want to remember it all.

"I'm sorry, Sergeant." Uncle Edward squeezed my shoulders. "I'm afraid Cissy can't be much help." He let go of me and shook the detective's hand. "We'll call you if she remembers anything more."

Sergeant Harman hesitated, then shrugged and let Uncle Edward lead him to the door. "We'll stay in touch, Mr. Crandall," he said. "We're close to cracking this and would appreciate any help you can give us."

"I'd keep an eye on her if I were you," I heard him add when they were on the porch. And Uncle Edward looked thoughtful for the rest of the evening.

They talked to Jake too. Called him down to the station and everything.

"Pa raged like an angry bull," Jake told me when he came over the next Saturday, "but they drug me down there anyway. Said I wasn't in any trouble, but I think they wanted to see if I knew anything about Roy Cummings's murder."

Jake couldn't tell them much either, although he did give them a better description of the other man. "They seemed happier after that," Jake said, "and treated me with more respect when I told them how I nearly beat him in a fight that day in front of Gimble's."

I cringed when I remembered Jake's broken face. I wanted to say I was proud of him. I really was, but not for fighting, so I didn't say anything at all.

Jake left later than usual that night. He didn't have to be home until eleven o'clock, which worked out fine because I had to be in the house by ten and it was an hour drive from our house in San Bernardino to his in Highland Park. Uncle Edward and Aunt Rose were in the living room when I walked Jake out to his father's truck.

The crickets were singing in the ivy and a full summer moon lit up the yard like floodlights on a stage. Jake hugged me anyway, long and hard. I thought he'd never let me go. And then he kissed me. A real kiss, soft and warm and almost desperate.

He never said another word except good-by, and I thought I saw his eyes tear up when he shut the door and backed slowly down the driveway.

Chapter
Five

Jake's younger brother Tim called me in July. "Jake's gone," he said over the hum of the long-distance wire. "He's run away and Ma said I should call and see if you know where he is."

I couldn't think what to say. I hadn't heard from Jake since June when he'd kissed me good-by that Saturday night. I thought it was strange he didn't call or write. What if Roy Cummings's cronies got hold of him and he was rotting in a fish barrel too? But Uncle Edward said, "Don't worry, honey, if anything were wrong we'd know."

They hadn't let me call him. Long distance was expensive, and "besides," Aunt Rose insisted, "it's not proper for a young lady to call a boy."

I looked over at Mary Margaret and she stared daggers, daring me to tell. She called Wesley Harris all the time, but his number wasn't long distance so her parents couldn't know. I kept quiet. It wouldn't help for me to ruin her love life too. Besides, if Aunt Rose found out, she'd be grounded to our room and I'd never have any privacy.

When Tim called, I told him I didn't know where Jake had gone. Tim said he'd taken off the Saturday before after a blowup with their pa. "Pa wanted Jake to get a job on weekends too.

Said how driving back and forth to another county was a waste of time and gas. He told Jake, 'There's plenty of girls for you to date right here in L.A.' And hid the car keys."

Tim talked longer than he should have. He told me he'd turned fourteen in March and how he'd always liked me best of all the girls in the old neighborhood. "I could come and see you, Cissy. If Jake don't, that is."

Jake had shown me a snap of him and Tim standing in the yard next to the hedge where Jake and I used to stand and talk. Tim looked a lot like Jake, except just a little shorter. And Tim had green eyes instead of brown. I loved Jake's eyes. They could dance or brood without a second in between.

I could never think of Tim as anything but Jake's pest of a little brother. I didn't tell him that, of course. I knew there wasn't much chance of him coming clear down to see me.

I don't remember what I did say. I remember hanging up and feeling cold all over. Aunt Rose got out the thermometer and shut the window in my room. "I hope you're not coming down with a summer cold," she fretted and handed me a glass of lemonade.

It wasn't a cold I was worried about; it was Jake. Where could he have gone? And didn't he know I'd be worried?

By the time I heard from him three weeks later, I was in such a stew I could hardly think straight.

I got a letter one Monday afternoon in August. The postman chuckled when he handed it to Aunt Rose and tipped his hat when he saw me standing behind her in the doorway. "Hello, beautiful," he said with a wink before walking off down the sidewalk whistling.

Aunt Rose smiled too when she handed me the letter. Then I saw what they were laughing at. The letter was addressed to "My Beautiful Darling Girl." And I recognized Jake's handwriting right away.

I didn't wait for Aunt Rose to shut the screen. I took off for the bathroom and locked myself in. Mary Margaret was at the library; at least, that's where she'd told Aunt Rose she was going, but the door to our room didn't have a lock and I didn't want to be disturbed just then.

"Dear Cissy," the letter said. Why couldn't he have saved the "beautiful" part for the inside? "I'm sorry not to call or write you sooner. I wish I could have seen you one more time, but it wasn't possible. I had a ride to San Diego and who knows how long it would have took to find another."

San Diego? I felt a thrill of excitement and fear. San Diego was a Navy town. *He'd never!* I told myself and scanned the letter for a clue. Sure enough, there it was in the second paragraph right after: "I can't stay home and take Pa's bossing any longer.

"I joined the Navy, Cissy. Being a boot is hard, but they promised to make a man of me and I won't let them down. It's my chance to see the world and make something of myself."

He went on to say how after training he would go to sea on a carrier and later learn to fly the planes. "I'll be home again someday, babe. Then we'll talk about the future. Yours and mine. I'll be an Ace and make lots of money and support you in style."

I read the last part over and over until I had it memorized. I couldn't take it in. Was he asking me to wait for him? Did he want to marry me someday?

My heart was pounding and I couldn't see for tears. Aunt Rose knocked softly on the bathroom door. "Are you all right, sweetheart? Is Jake okay?"

"I'm all right," I lied. I hid the letter in my pocket and blew my nose. I waited a few minutes before opening the door, but Aunt Rose was still there. She took one look at me and knew things weren't okay, so I told her where Jake had gone and let her hold me till my tears dried up.

That night Uncle Edward called Jake's father, but they'd already heard. "He wrote us too," Mr. Freeman said. "The kid's got guts, I'll give him that. Good to talk to you, Crandall."

"And he hung up. Just like that! I'll tell you, Rose," Uncle Edward snorted, "I'd run away from that man too."

"Edward!" Aunt Rose nodded in my direction, but Uncle Edward just patted my shoulder and went off to his room. I knew he'd spend a little time alone and come back out his old self.

* * *

By the time school started up again, Sam and I were friends again. He'd avoided me for weeks after the Backward Dance, wouldn't look at me in class or joke when we met at our locker. When summer came, his folks took him to New York to visit family. Then one day in September he threw a gum wrapper at me across the table in the lunchroom and I knew it was all okay. He took me to the movies and school dances our whole sophomore year and sometimes tried to kiss me goodnight.

"It's a challenge," Mary Margaret nodded wisely when I told her. "Guys like to make a game of things like that. Let him kiss you once and have it over with. Then he'll calm down, and *maybe* you can just be friends."

"What do you mean, 'maybe'? We *are* just friends." I didn't like the idea that Sam might still think he had a chance with me.

Mary Margaret shrugged. "You lead him on, Cissy. If you let him take you out all the time he's bound to think there's a spark of interest there. Besides"—she tugged on the collar of her new white blouse and smoothed the waistband on her skirt—"it wouldn't hurt to keep a boyfriend in reserve." She turned and looked me in the eye. "Face it, Cissy, you don't know when Jake will be home. And when he does come back he'll probably have changed." She turned back to the mirror. "Anyway, you know what they say about sailors. They're sure to have a girl in every port."

"Wesley is a sailor," I reminded her, and felt my ears and neck heat up. She had no right to talk about Jake that way!

Wesley had graduated in June of 1937 and joined the Navy that September. He'd been accepted into Officers Training School, and the way Mary Margaret carried on, you'd have thought he'd been commissioned a duke.

Back then, Mary Margaret still had six months of school to go, and Uncle Edward insisted she finish. "No daughter of mine will quit school to get married, so you can put that right out of your head, young lady." She knew he meant business, so she told Wesley they would have to wait, and she went back to Central High.

If she had heard the break in my voice she ignored it and smiled at the mirror. "Wesley's different," she said and marched out of the room.

Even though she'd hurt my feelings, I decided to give her advice a try and let Sam kiss me.

It was prom night, May 1938. They wouldn't let two sophomores in the dance, so Sam suggested we see a movie.

"*The Good Earth* is playing at the Tower," he shouted over the static on our telephone. One of the older ladies on our party line kept trying to dial through, so I just hollered, "I'll be ready at seven," and hung up.

I didn't tell him I went just to see if I would understand the movie better than I did the book. Some parts I did, and some I didn't. I just thought the whole thing was so sad.

After the movie, we walked to Louie's and ordered ice cream sodas. Sam had vanilla and I ordered strawberry. I really liked chocolate best, but chocolate was the flavor malt I'd shared with Jake, and I didn't want to be reminded of that when I was with another boy. Even if it was only Sam.

We got off the bus on the corner of Fourth and Sherwood Lane. I let Sam hold my hand all the way home. I could feel him begin to sweat a block away, and I knew he was thinking about trying to kiss me good-night.

Maybe Mary Margaret's right, I thought. *Maybe I should let him kiss me and get it over with.* I began to sweat some too.

The moon slid silently behind a cloud just as we reached the porch. Sam let go of my hand and wiped his palm on his good slacks. I scrunched up my handkerchief to dry mine, and when he leaned toward me I didn't turn away.

I don't know who was more surprised—Sam, whose mouth met mine, then slid away and landed on my chin, or Aunt Rose, who chose that moment to open the front door and call Tarzan, our big gray tomcat, in for the night.

I didn't say a thing to either of them for two days. By then I'd gotten over my embarrassment and worked up the nerve to tell Sam I couldn't date him unless he agreed to quit playing games.

"I don't want to be a challenge anymore," I told him at the locker on Monday morning. "I just want to be your friend."

Sam looked confused. "It's okay, Cissy," he stammered. "We *are* friends. Heck, you're still the best dancer at Central High." He grinned. "Besides, none of the other girls would sit through *The Good Earth* and share their popcorn too."

Chapter
Six

Mary Margaret had graduated in February with the winter class of '38. She wouldn't turn eighteen until August, but Wesley came home and married her in June.

Being around Wesley made me uncomfortable. He was tall and slender with swarthy skin and stormy eyes that darted around the room whenever we talked to him. He was handsome and knew it.

"He always acts like he'd rather be somewhere else," Billy said once. And I realized he was right.

Aunt Rose had a fit when they told her and Uncle Edward their plans. "What do you mean, a justice of the peace?" Her voice rose an octave higher with each word, and she grabbed ahold of Uncle Edward's arm to steady herself. When she caught her breath she sounded determined.

"You'll do no such thing. If you insist on getting married, Pastor Stewart can do the ceremony. September will be soon enough. You can get another leave by then, can't you, Wesley?"

Wesley wore his dress blues proudly. He stood stiff and proper by the front room window, hands tucked behind his back like a guard at Buckingham Palace. He stared straight ahead and pretended not to hear. Uncle Edward looked like he wanted to throttle him.

Aunt Rose was still holding Uncle Edward's arm when she tried again with Mary Margaret. "Don't be foolish, darling, you must wait for a real wedding. If you do this now, I'm afraid you'll look back and wish you'd waited."

Mary Margaret's face was almost purple. She formed her lips into a stubborn pout and linked her arm with Wesley's. "We're getting married, Mother," her eyes sparked in defiance, "with or without your permission."

"Go to your room, young lady!" Uncle Edward bellowed. But Mary Margaret wouldn't budge.

I did, though. I grabbed Billy by the sleeve and dragged him up the stairs. We sat in his room with the door cracked open and listened. The argument went on half the night, with Aunt Rose and Uncle Edward sounding angry then reasonable by turns. Mary Margaret wouldn't give an inch, and Wesley stayed silent.

Finally, Uncle Edward called a halt.

The clock chimed midnight. Billy had fallen asleep with Tarzan on his chest. The house was quiet for so long I thought Mary Margaret and Wesley had gone. Then I heard Uncle Edward say, "All right. I'll not let this destroy our family. Let's all go to bed and settle the details in the morning."

I could hear Aunt Rose's quiet sobs as she climbed the stairs, and I made a beeline for my bed. I pretended to be asleep so I wouldn't have to talk to Mary Margaret, but by the time she came up half an hour later, I was drifting off to sleep for real.

* * *

Once they accepted the idea, everyone pitched in to help with the wedding. Aunt Rose even recruited our neighbor Carl Long.

Captain Long was a retired Navy man. He had served his country during the Great War and talked about "the Big One" to anyone who would listen. Billy would listen for hours, but

Mary Margaret and I tried to stay out of his way. His stories were either boring or, as he often told us, "too bold for delicate ears." If Aunt Rose had known how bold his stories really were, Billy wouldn't have been listening either.

Captain Long was a great gardener, though. Aunt Rose insisted he had two green thumbs. "How a man like that can grow roses that size I'll never know!" she said one night while they were playing cards with the Hendersons.

Uncle Edward laid down his meld. "Must be the fertilizer." He kept a straight face, but Mr. Henderson laughed so hard I thought he'd choke.

Anyway, Captain Long had roses and baby's breath and lots of other things in bloom that would make a wedding a true joy to see. "Help yourself, dear lady," he told Aunt Rose. "My garden is yours to purloin."

The wedding went off without a hitch. Mary Margaret looked spectacular in an ankle-length dress with ivory lace. Aunt Rose had stitched some netting to a beadwork headband for a veil and borrowed roses from the captain to make the bride's bouquet.

I stood on Mary Margaret's left side with my own nosegay and the groom's ring. Billy and Uncle Edward each wore a white carnation in the lapel of their Sunday suits, and Billy handed Wesley Mary Margaret's ring. Aunt Rose wore a gardenia corsage and held tight to a lace hankie. I thought the flowers should last forever; they'd been watered by so many tears.

The bride and groom drove off to the Ambassador Hotel in Wesley's Buick for a two-day honeymoon. Then Wesley brought Mary Margaret home to Uncle Edward's and went back to sea.

Things were pretty awkward after that. Mary Margaret and I shared a room, but didn't talk much. She moped around, face drawn and teary-eyed. Aunt Rose and Uncle Edward tried to treat her the same as always, but we all knew things weren't right.

For my part, I didn't understand how Mary Margaret could treat her own parents with such disrespect. Didn't she know how lucky she was to have folks who loved her and wanted to take care of her? She didn't know what it was like to be without a family and a home. She'd never watched her sister die, or lived in an orphanage or had to cook and clean and watch little children for her keep. She'd never had her brother and baby sister taken away, or her father executed, or seen her mother talk to people who weren't there.

By the time I'd had a day or two to stew about it, I had myself so worked up I could hardly be civil to anyone.

Poor Billy, I made him the target for my tirade. He said I made his ears hurt and I should just tell Mary Margaret what a selfish, spoiled pig she was, and why he had to live in a house with a bunch of stupid females he'd never know. He slammed his bedroom door and almost chopped off Tarzan's tail. Tarzan hid in the garage for a week.

If Aunt Rose noticed our behavior, she kept it to herself. She read her Bible every morning, and I knew Uncle Edward went up an hour early every night to pray.

After several days of misery, I decided to do some praying of my own.

It was one of those nights that stay light forever. The clock on the stove said a quarter to nine, but the temperature still felt like noon. I took a glass of lemonade out to the porch and watched a huge summer moon chase the sun out of the sky.

I thought about the psalm Uncle Edward had read aloud that morning. *The Lord is my Shepherd; I shall not want. He maketh me to lie down in green pastures: he leadeth me beside the still waters . . .* I sighed. Such a peaceful thought.

My heart was anything but at peace. I resented Mary Margaret for upsetting our happy home. I felt angry that she had married her beloved Wesley but I hadn't even talked to Jake in months. Worse yet, all the memories I had so carefully packed away had dragged themselves out into the open again.

I guess if I had been honest I would have said I was mad at God about that. Why'd he let it happen? Didn't the Bible say he knew everything ahead of time? It would seem to me he could have prevented all of this, or at the very least protected me from memories best left alone.

The blood thudded painfully in my chest. I knew I was getting ready to cry again and I didn't want to.

As the last mockingbird called good-night from the eucalyptus tree, a soft breeze cooled my forehead and ruffled the hair on my arms. I lifted my face and stared at an aura of light that suddenly surrounded the moon. It was as if the hand of God had touched my cheek and caused me to look up at him.

I felt my heartbeat slow, then closed my eyes.

Chapter
Seven

I felt better after that night, but Mary Margaret and I still didn't talk much for a while. She was listless and unhappy, helping with chores only when she absolutely had to.

I had never known Aunt Rose to be anything but kind and gentle. She went out of her way to please and care for us and Uncle Edward. She was usually patient and seldom put her foot down about anything. But this time she did—right in the middle of Mary Margaret's back.

I didn't hear what happened until months later when Mary Margaret and I were friends again. But one morning in July, Mary Margaret came downstairs an hour late for breakfast, still in her nightgown and robe. She hadn't washed her hair in a week, and her slippers looked like she'd been stomping in a mud puddle.

She plopped down at the kitchen table like the queen of Sheba and watched me dry the last of the dishes. "There's no French toast left," she whined. "I can't believe you didn't save me any breakfast. I'm sure Cissy and Billy got everything they wanted."

It was on the tip of my tongue to tell her, "Be careful, you'll trip on your lip," when Aunt Rose threw the dish rag in the sink and turned around.

"Cissy," she said calmly, "please go upstairs and strip the beds. We need to wash sheets today."

I looked at the two of them. Aunt Rose had Mary Margaret's full attention, and I knew I'd be better off anyplace else.

"Yes, ma'am," I said and hurried up the stairs.

* * *

Things got better after that. Mary Margaret picked up her things, helped around the house and tried not to be so surly. Still, I think we were all relieved when Wesley wrote to say he'd been promoted and assigned to better duty at the Navy base in San Pedro. He'd found a flat for them in Long Beach. "A small apartment over a garage," he wrote. "But it's clean and it will do until I can put some money aside." He came for her September first, the day before my sixteenth birthday.

I helped her pack some boxes with sheets and towels and a cast iron skillet she'd gotten for a wedding gift. "What kind of present is this?" She'd scowled when she opened the box. But Aunt Rose told her she'd be grateful later when she discovered how much she'd use it.

Mary Margaret folded some sweaters and put them in the suitcase Uncle Edward had found in the attic. It had belonged to Grandma Eva a long time ago. "I know she'd want you to have it," was all Uncle Edward said. Later, I found out it was the suitcase Grandma Eva had loaned him when he and Aunt Rose first moved away.

"Here, Cissy," Mary Margaret said when she got to the bottom of her sweater drawer. "Would you like to have this for a birthday present?"

She handed me a white evening bag stitched with iridescent sequins and tiny seed pearls. It was the prettiest bag I'd ever seen.

"Oh, dear," I gasped. "Mary Margaret, it's beautiful. How can you bear to part with it?"

She shrugged. "Mama gave it to me when I was sixteen, remember? I'll probably never use it again.

"Anyway," she went on, brightening, "I'm sure Wesley will buy me new things when we get settled." She kissed my cheek and hurried out the door, but not before I saw the worry in her eyes.

*   *   *

I was worried too, but not for Mary Margaret. I didn't know enough about Wesley then to be scared for her. It was Jake that kept me wide awake at night. It was Jake I prayed for on my knees beside my bed and in my back-porch talks with God. I'd heard from him just twice that summer. Once in June, after he got my letter about Mary Margaret and Wesley getting married, and once in August, just a week before my birthday. That letter came in a birthday card.

"To My Sweet Sixteen," it read. "Hope you're having fun. Did Sam take you to the Fourth of July picnic? Tell Billy I miss our baseball games.

"I've been assigned to a battleship, the USS *West Virginia*. My CO says if I bust my rear, I might impress someone who can get me on a Carrier. For now I'm stuck greasing the engines and cleaning the muck out of spare parts. I'm not worried, though. I'll be a pilot someday, just wait."

He went on to say nothing much was new and he didn't know when he'd be home. The card was signed "Love, Jake," but somehow those words didn't sound as hopeful as they once did.

Aunt Rose never asked to read my letters, but she did hang around after I got one to see if everything was all right. "How's Jake?" she asked after I'd opened the birthday card and spent half an hour in my room.

I shrugged. "He's okay, I guess. Oh, Aunt Rose, do you think he'll ever get back home again?"

She hugged me hard and patted my cheek. "Of course he will, sweetheart. I know it seems like he's been gone forever, but school starts next week and time will fly. You'll see."

I thought she understood until I heard her talking to Uncle Edward in the kitchen after dinner.

"We have to encourage Cissy to date other boys, Edward."

"Why on earth would we do that?" Uncle Edward sounded annoyed, and I knew he was still upset about Wesley and Mary Margaret.

Aunt Rose sighed. "Because she's counting too much on Jake, that's why." I could hear her stacking dishes in the sink and Uncle Edward's paper rattle as he turned the page. "What if Jake never comes back? Edward, please put that paper down!"

I heard a chair scrape the linoleum as she sat down. Uncle Edward cleared his throat, but I didn't stay around long enough to hear what else they said.

My room felt cold, even though the thermometer said eighty degrees. I kicked off my shoes and crawled under the sheet and bedspread on my bed. *What if Jake never comes home?* The question raged through my ears and thudded with the pounding of my heart. *Never home . . . Never home . . . Never home . . .*

* * *

Aunt Rose was right about two things: school did start and time did fly.

I joined the glee club at school and the choir at church. Everyone said I had a nice voice. "It might not make Mary Lou jealous," Dotty said one day in my junior year, "but your voice is better than Donna's and you're a shoo-in for the school play."

Donna and I were both altos and both finalists in the tryouts for the three good fairies in the play, *Sleeping Beauty*. Mary Lou was the glee club's lead soprano and she already had her part sealed. Our director, Miss Gregors, insisted Mary Lou could make the ground shake with her throaty high C.

I thought she had a good voice but would have said she sounded more like a screech owl on a note that high.

Dotty had the part of the second fairy, and it was up to Miss Gregors to choose me or Donna for the third. Mr. Atkins, my algebra teacher, played the prince, and he had to kiss Miss Gregors in the last act. I wanted to be around to see that every day at practice.

Donna missed two notes at the tryouts. But I woke up that morning with a cold and sounded like a stepped-on frog.

Miss Gregors was sympathetic. "I'm sorry, Cissy, but we have to start rehearsal right away. I'm afraid I don't have time to give you another chance."

Dotty acted like she'd bust a gizzard. "I can't believe Miss Gregors gave the part to Donna," she fumed. "You're much better than she is, and your cold will be gone in a week."

Dotty didn't like Donna very much. Donna had stolen her tenth-grade boyfriend, then bragged around the school how he'd ditched Dotty for her because she had fuller lips. She had a big head too, and I knew it would be hard for them to practice together.

I wasn't too disappointed after I found out that Mr. Atkins would only kiss Miss Gregors once, the night of the play. The drama coach said they could fake it till then. Dotty said everyone booed and hissed but couldn't make them change their minds.

Sam and I got front-row seats on opening night. Dotty and Donna sang together fine, and Mary Lou only hit one sour note. When the prince came riding in on a fake white horse everybody held their breath. He wandered through the castle trying not to step on any of the cast who lay around pretending to be asleep, while the three good fairies made swishing motions from behind to hurry him along.

He found Sleeping Beauty in her attic room lying still as death on clean white sheets. Everyone held their breath again as he stared at her, pure love beaming from his face. In one motion he swept off his hat, knelt beside the bed and bent his head to hers. He stayed like that a minute, his eyes saying things I could only guess at. Then he touched his lips to hers in a kiss that seemed to last forever. The audience roared as Miss Gregors sat up looking mystified, then happy when she saw her prince.

Later, when he walked me home, Sam asked me why I'd cried.

Chapter
Eight

Before I knew it, Easter was over and May was just around the corner. Two boys had asked me to the junior dance, but I told them "sorry" and went with Sam like always. Everyone but Dotty and a few others thought that Sam and I were an item. Even Aunt Rose and Uncle Edward began to watch us closer and ask Sam silly questions like, "What do you plan to do after graduation, and does your family attend temple services?" Once they even invited Sam and his parents to dinner. Sam said they would have come, but his father had to go out of town on business.

Sam's father was a butcher, so I thought that was probably a lie. But I was grateful anyway. Sam's mother was nice enough, but I didn't want her to get the wrong idea about Sam and me. Aunt Rose and Uncle Edward had good intentions, they just fussed too much.

Two days after the junior dance, our family pulled into the driveway after church and a car pulled in right behind us.

"Well, I'll be," Uncle Edward said into the rearview mirror.

"Who is it, Edward?" Aunt Rose turned around to get a better look.

"It's Jake!" Billy shouted, and they all piled out of the car.

I sat still as stone. The world went black, then gold, then light enough to see the scratch by the ashtray in the back seat where Billy had nicked it with his pocketknife. Next thing I knew, Jake was standing by the open car door.

"What's wrong, babe, aren't you glad to see me?"

Glad? I wanted to jump in his arms and hug him, and smack him and break his nose again—all at once.

I guess I must have looked as confused as I felt. Jake set down his bag, reached into the car and pulled me out.

"Surprised you, didn't I?" He grinned and kept hold of my hand.

Uncle Edward talked to the driver of the other car while Billy fumbled with the latchkey at the front door. "Come into the house, you two," Aunt Rose called from the porch. "You can visit while I make lunch."

I don't remember what we said. Not the words, anyway. Jake told me he had thirty days of liberty but had wasted almost a week hitchhiking to get there. He hadn't even been home to see his parents yet.

Dinner was a blur. Next thing I knew, we were headed out of town in Uncle Edward's car.

Jake whistled as he drove, a tune I'd never heard. But before I could ask what it was, he turned his head and grinned at me. "You're awfully quiet, Cissy. Where would you like to go?"

"To the lake." It came out without a thought from me. Later I was glad it had.

The water glistened in the sunlight. Unlike the time we'd been there before, there were other people around. Two other couples and a family having a picnic dinner.

We made our way down the rocks to the water's edge and walked about half a mile to a small white beach. There was a hot dog stand, not open yet, and a plywood shanty with three rowboats inside. No one was around. Jake called, "Hello. Anybody here?" But the only answer was his own voice echoing across the lake.

The other people were out of sight above the rocks. We could hear their chatter, then car doors slammed, an engine started, and they drove away.

Jake was poking around among the boats. "Here, Cissy," he said, "come grab this end."

"We can't!" I gasped and tried to stop him, but he already had the boat in the water. I started to giggle. "You goose! What if somebody comes?" But I took his arm and let him help me into the rocking boat. "What if it leaks?"

Suddenly I didn't care. So what if we got arrested for stealing someone else's boat? So what if we sank in the middle of the lake and had to swim for shore? Jake was back. I felt happy and free—more alive than I had felt in a very long time.

* * *

Jake spent the night on the living-room sofa, and his pa came to get him after work on Monday afternoon. Aunt Rose let me stay home from school, but Jake spent most of the day doing yard chores. Aunt Rose never asked him to do a thing, but Jake said he wanted to help out as a thank you "for dinner and a bed, and the use of the car." He smiled at me when he said that and I blushed, but no one else saw.

Billy was the one who should have felt "thanked." Jake trimmed the ivy, turned the garden soil, and painted the mailbox—all chores Billy was supposed to do on Saturday. I didn't mind, though. It gave Jake and me time to be together and talk.

We saw each other twice more before he went back to the ship. Toward the end of May we went to the lake, but the hot dog stand was open and there were more people around. A surly old man with a white mustache rented us the same boat we'd used for free two weeks before.

"A dollar an hour," he growled, "and don't lose the oars."

Jake paid him the dollar, but it just wasn't the same, and we came in after forty-five minutes.

The breeze had picked up, and a warm spring drizzle sent people scurrying for cover. Jake and I climbed the rocks and sat on the edge looking over the lake. He held a blanket around us. "To keep us dry," he said.

After a minute his hand closed around my arm, and he drew me closer. I leaned my head against his shoulder and wished I could stay like that forever, feeling his breath against my hair and the rhythm of his heart beneath my cheek.

* * *

On a brilliant morning, the first of June, I watched him walk away. A bus would take him to the depot where he'd catch a train for San Diego, and the Navy would own him for another two years.

The others had said their good-bys and were out back working in the garden. I was glad no one was there to see me. I felt like someone had kicked me in the stomach, sick and sore and all used up inside. I couldn't cry. Not yet, anyway.

"Wait for me, Cissy," he had said, "I'll be back before you know it."

Later, I'd find comfort in those words, those words and our good-by kiss. A kiss that held promises I knew we'd both do our best to keep.

Chapter
Nine

To tell the truth, I hadn't thought about Roy Cummings and his friends in months. Uncle Edward never talked about them, and that bothersome detective hadn't been back. We knew the police had arrested a man just a few weeks after they talked to Jake and me, but we never heard if he'd been convicted or not.

Then in January of 1940, halfway through my senior year, Uncle Edward came home early from work.

I heard the car pull in the drive and felt a jolt of fear. For some reason, I remembered the time Papa came home early back in Pike and all the trouble that came after that.

Aunt Rose turned off the iron and met Uncle Edward at the door.

"What is it, Edward? Are you ill?"

I could understand why she would ask that. He looked like he'd wrestled with a ghost and lost. His face was gray, his hair mussed up, and the buttons on his jacket were all undone.

He took Aunt Rose's hand away from his forehead and held on for dear life. "Will you please excuse us, Cissy?" he said. "I want to talk to Rose alone."

His voice was raspy, like he had a cold, but I knew he didn't and that scared me even more. I set aside the book I'd been reading for English, picked up Tarzan and headed outside.

Tarzan was indignant at having his nap disturbed. I must have held him too tight, because he bit my thumb and ran under the wisteria licking furiously at his fur.

It had been a long time since I'd climbed a tree, but right then a tree seemed the safest place to be, so I grabbed hold of the lowest limb of the apple tree and hauled myself into the branches. I felt dizzy at first, then cold. The leaves were still damp from last night's rain.

Our eucalyptus stood only a few feet away, and the smell made me sneeze. It was a while before I calmed down enough to see how stupid I was acting. Here I was, seventeen years old, almost out of school and hiding from trouble in a tree like a frightened cub.

"Cissy Marie," I scolded myself, "you haven't got the sense God gave a goose. There's no reason to feel so afraid."

But there was. There really was.

When our family had something serious to discuss, Uncle Edward usually called a meeting around the kitchen table. But if someone was in trouble, he and Aunt Rose called the culprit (usually Billy) into their room and shut the door. Billy then would come out red-faced and sometimes teary-eyed, and that would be the end of the matter.

I had just made up my mind to slide back down the tree when Uncle Edward came to the back door.

"Cissy," he called. "Will you come in here a minute, please? We need to talk to you."

A sharp twig stung my shin and the tree bark scraped my palms. When I walked into the living room Aunt Rose took my hand. She looked pale. It hit me then, as it had once before, that someone must have died.

Mama. My heart twisted. *Oh, God, please don't let it be.*

"It's Mama, isn't it?" I gasped. "Is she . . . ?"

"No, Cissy. Lynetta is fine." Uncle Edward shut the bedroom door behind us and motioned me to sit on the end of their bed.

Dust motes danced in a beam of sunlight from the open window. When I was little I loved to watch them sparkle. "Fairy dust," Papa had explained back then. "It's magic, and only good little girls ever get to see it." Papa always knew how to make me feel special.

Uncle Edward clasped his hands behind his back and began to pace the floor. "Cissy, remember what you told us about Roy Cummings—how he hung around your house and watched your father come and go?"

"Have you seen anybody else like that?" Aunt Rose broke in. "Not Roy, of course, but another man—hanging around here, I mean. Oh, dear, I'm handling this badly." She looked up helplessly. "Edward?"

Uncle Edward cleared his throat and came around to face me. "Cissy, another man has been killed. One of the foremen at the plant. He was the union representative for his department, and Sergeant Harman thinks he was murdered by the same people who killed Berdowski."

I shook my head. "I don't understand. Why would that have anything to do with me?" I couldn't see how any of us could be in danger. The man who saw me, the one with Roy in the alley, couldn't possibly know where I was; I'd moved around too much. Anyway, that was more than three years ago.

"Harman thinks the man you saw in the alley with Roy is involved in this case too." He looked at Aunt Rose, then back at me. "He also thinks you're in danger."

"Edward." Aunt Rose's voice held a note of warning.

"She needs to hear this, Rose. We can't chaperon her all day long." He turned back to me. "Cissy, there was a note on my desk. Harman has it now, but it said 'Curiosity killed the cats.' Detective Harman thinks it was a warning for you and Jake.

Possibly us as well." Uncle Edward went quiet.

Aunt Rose took my hand. "Cissy, there may be nothing to worry about, but you need to pay attention at school, the movies, wherever you are. If you see anything or anyone that looks suspicious, you run. Hear me?" She squeezed my shoulders. "And don't go anywhere alone. Not anywhere."

Her fingers dug into my back, but I didn't move. I nodded and she let me go, but I couldn't think what it all meant.

Was I really in danger? I couldn't identify anybody. Jake could, but he was out to sea; surely nothing could happen to him there.

Sergeant Harman came back the next day and handed me his card. "Anytime, anyplace, you call me. Even if you think it might be a mistake. You let me be the judge—got it?"

"Yes," I said and tried to sound polite, but I could feel my hackles rise.

"Some men are otters and some are porcupines," Grandma Eva told me once. "One is smooth and charming, the other's always pricking folks without even trying."

I decided the detective was a porcupine.

* * *

I went everywhere with either Dotty or Sam. Sometimes both. But weeks went by and nothing happened. I wrote to Jake and he wrote back to say the police had contacted him too, through the commander's office, no less!

"Boy, they sure know how to scare a guy," he told me. "I thought I was headed for the brig. But don't you worry, Cissy. There's no way they can touch me. Not here, anyway. It's you I'm worried about. Be careful, babe. If anything happened to you, I'd have to kill him. I really would."

My skin prickled when I read that part. *Would he really kill a man for me?* I pushed the thought away.

Jake went on to say how much he missed me and that he'd

be home in time for graduation.

"Can he stay here, Aunt Rose? Just one night, so we can go to the party."

Our class had a big party planned at the Palace Ballroom. We'd rented the whole room and it was ours till midnight. The graduation committee had been working for weeks. Dotty pestered Mary Lou until she told us there would even be a band.

"Of course, dear." Aunt Rose smoothed the slipcover on the sofa. "He can sleep down here like he did before."

Jake's coming home. Jake's coming home. The words played in my mind like a symphony. His face, his smile, the way his hair flopped down over his eyes when he was nervous or tired. Visions of Jake filled my dreams.

I was so caught up with graduation plans and thoughts of Jake, I almost said no when Sam asked me to a party at Donna's.

Donna's parties were usually boring. "There's no room," she'd say if someone suggested we dance. But I knew it was because she didn't know how to dance, and she only liked music she could sing to.

"Come on, Cissy." Sam sounded impatient. "We won't have a chance to go to parties much longer. Unless, of course, you change your mind and come with me to UCLA."

I could almost see him holding his breath on the other end of the phone line. He'd grown six inches in the last four years, and his shoes had gone up two sizes. He was still a good dancer. And handsome, even if his nose was just a smidgen too big. He had dark curly hair and skillet-black eyes that Dotty swore "could look right through you."

"Sam," I warned when he brought up college again.

"Okay, okay. Just Donna's then. I'll pick you up at seven."

Sam was always open and honest, and I was afraid he still held out hope that we'd have a future together. I couldn't understand why. I'd been blunt with him about my feelings for Jake. Yet he kept calling and taking me out. "You can't just sit around waiting," he insisted. "Jake should be thankful I'm taking care of you for him."

I smiled in spite of myself. How could I turn him down? I really liked Sam. It seemed like we'd been friends forever. And friends are like gold, Mama had told me: "The more you have on hand, the richer you are."

I realized she was right. My life was definitely richer because of Sam. And Dotty too, of course. I promised myself I'd push Jake to the back of my mind and just enjoy the company.

C h a p t e r
T e n

We played Monopoly till midnight.

"Oh, Sam," I howled when I saw the clock, "look at the time! Aunt Rose will have a fit."

"Should we call?" He handed Donna his paper money and started clearing off the board.

I knew we should. It had always been a rule to call if you were going to be late, but I'd never been this late and they were probably in bed already. I felt guilty remembering the nights Aunt Rose had waited up for Mary Margaret. The lines of worry on her face and the migraine headaches.

I shook my head. "I don't want to wake them. Besides, we're only a few blocks away. If we hurry, we'll be there before they could answer the phone." I grabbed my sweater and Sam's hand, and we were out the door in a flash.

We saw a car parked across the street from Donna's and heard it pull away from the curb when we were halfway down the block. It followed us all the way to Mountain Boulevard.

The side streets were deserted, and traffic on the boulevard was light. Sam pulled me along until I ran out of breath and had to stop at the corner of Mountain and First. Sherwood Drive was only one block down and one over. We slowed to a fast walk and Sam looked back.

"Isn't that the same car we saw outside Dotty's the other night?"

I turned to look and felt a stab of fear. "It was at Donna's when we got there, in the same spot across the street." I'd noticed because one of the men in the front seat had thrown a cigarette out the window just as we walked by.

The car pulled up right behind us and slowed to match our pace. *Like a panther stalking its prey.* I felt like a dozen panthers were sitting on my chest. My ears were ringing and I almost missed Sam's instructions.

"We're going to run for it, doll. When I say go, you move fast, okay?"

I gulped and nodded, but I was sure I couldn't run. My feet were lead and my lungs ached with every breath.

I heard the engine rev.

"GO!" Sam shouted above the roaring in my ears.

He took off, pulling me around the corner. Brakes squealed as the car careened after us. Our porch light shone like a beacon, only a few yards ahead.

Sam stopped like he'd hit a wall and shoved me hard into the hedge that protected Captain Long's garden. My head hit something hard. I rolled to my knees and scrunched up in a ball, waiting for Sam to dive in after me. Instead I heard the car pick up speed and then a sickening thud. I looked back through the broken hedge in time to see Sam's body roll along the sidewalk. He ended up sprawled face down beneath the maple tree.

He wasn't moving.

Oh, God, please don't let him be dead.

I felt dizzy. Something warm and sticky ran down my forehead into my eyes. "Sam!" I choked, then filled my lungs with air and tried again. *"Sam!"* He didn't answer.

What if they come back? I clawed my way back through the hedge. My hand closed around a large, jagged rock. Later, I realized it must have been responsible for the gash in my head, but at the time I only saw it as a weapon. I pulled it free of the soft earth and crawled out onto the sidewalk. Sam lay only a few feet away, but I couldn't seem to make my body move another inch. I heard voices, then shouts and feet pounding on the hard cement.

We're both dying, I thought, as if I were someone else looking out of my own body. My eyes stung, but I felt an icy calm as a blurry form bent over Sam's body, then turned and moved toward me. I clenched my fist around the rock, praying, willing strength into my hand.

"Cissy! Don't move, sweetheart, an ambulance will be here soon." I let myself collapse into Uncle Edward's arms.

*   *   *

It's funny how we take things for granted—things and people too. Sam was always there: at our locker, in class, at parties and dances. Even when I told him to go away or hung up on him, he waited patiently for me to come around.

I thought I might never see him again and it was all my fault.

"You mustn't let it eat on you so," Aunt Rose insisted as she wrung out another cool rag and placed it on my forehead. The gash in my scalp would heal with the help of five stitches, but what about Sam? If he died . . . I knew I'd never forgive myself.

They wouldn't let me see him.

"He's still unconscious," Uncle Edward told me when I was awake enough to ask. "He wouldn't even know you were there. Just rest now. Sam's going to be all right. And you can't do a thing for him until you're well yourself."

That was a fact I could attest to every time I tried to move. My body felt like I'd been run over by a train. It looked like it too, with purple welts and scratches covering me from my head to my ankles. "Even my hair hurts," I told Dotty when she came to visit.

She and Donna popped in on the third morning after the "accident," as they called it, with cookies, a new novel and a copy of the *Panther Press,* our school paper.

"You're famous." Donna handed me the paper. "You and Sam made headlines."

"And not just in the school paper either." Dotty pulled out copies of the *Examiner* and *Tribune* from March 2.

There it was on the third page from the front:

HIT-AND-RUN DRIVER SERIOUSLY INJURES BOY
Seventeen-year-old Samuel Levi was critically injured in an early-morning hit-and-run accident

There was that word again. "It wasn't an accident," I said.

"What?" Dotty grabbed the paper back. "What do you mean 'it wasn't an accident'? Who would want to hurt Sam on purpose?"

The door opened, and Aunt Rose hustled the girls out into the hall. "You can come back tomorrow, Dorothy," I heard her tell Dotty. "Cissy needs to sleep now."

She came back upstairs a few minutes later with a brush and comb and a glass of orange juice. "Drink this, sweetheart." She handed me the glass and began to comb some of the knots out of my hair.

"Ow! Aunt Rose, what are you doing? I can do that later."

She hadn't combed my hair since I was fourteen and we had tried a new style. I couldn't figure why she thought she had to do it now.

She stopped and handed me the comb. "I didn't mean to upset you, dear, but Sergeant Harman is on his way over."

I stiffened and lowered the comb. "Now," she said, patting my arm, "I know you don't like him, but he has to ask you some questions. We have to find those men, Cissy." Then she added, "Uncle Edward will be home soon."

"What?"

"I called him. He wants to be here when they question you. I know it's hard, darling, but please cooperate." She picked up the brush and started on my hair again. "Those men have to be put behind bars or none of us will ever feel safe."

She's treating me like a five-year-old! I thought to myself, vowing to never get sick or injured again.

Uncle Edward must have said something to Detective Harman, because he was a little nicer to me this time. He nodded a lot and took notes in a small black notebook.

"Can you think of anything else about them?" he asked after I'd given him a pretty good description of the car and its two occupants. "Anything at all, even if it doesn't seem important."

It was hard to think. I didn't want to remember the brakes or the thud of Sam's body hitting the sidewalk, so I thought back to before that, when we'd seen the car the first time at Dotty's.

"He smokes."

Harman's pen stopped in midair. "Who smokes?"

"The man in the car. Not the driver, but the other one. He threw a cigarette out the window just as we walked by."

The detective looked at the young policeman standing next to him. "See about it, Carlson."

The young man nodded and left the room.

Detective Harman followed him a few minutes later and said good-by to Aunt Rose and Uncle Edward in the hall.

Two days later Sam woke up and talked his head off. He identified the driver from some snapshots. The police arrested the culprits a week later at a bar in San Diego.

But I couldn't keep myself from wondering, *Were those men in San Diego looking for Jake?* The thought made my stomach sick.

Chapter
Eleven

I'll never forget the morning of March 7, because it was the first day we knew for sure Sam was going to make it. There was a rainstorm too. A gully-washer that filled the storm drains and caused the gutters to flood up over the curbs.

By the time Aunt Rose got me to the hospital, afternoon visiting hours were over. But Sergeant Harman and his partner were just leaving, so I slipped into the room while Aunt Rose talked to them at the nurses' station.

Sam was lying on his back, wrapped in bandages from head to toe, his plastered legs hanging from hooks above the bed. One arm was bent and strapped to his chest with more white bandages.

"Hi, doll." His voice cracked on the words. My throat closed off, and it was a minute before I could answer.

"Oh, Sam," I finally croaked, "what have they done to you?"

He tried to smile, but I could see the pain in his eyes. "Got me good, didn't they? Are you all right?"

"I'm fine, really. Please don't worry about me."

I fished a hankie out of the pocket of my skirt. "Oh, Sam, I'm so sorry. It was me they were after. You shouldn't have even been involved."

He reached out and grabbed my hand. "Hush. It's all right, I'd do it again in a minute." He took a deep breath and grimaced at the pain. "I love you, Cissy, you know that."

"I love you too, Sam. I mean . . ."

He gave my hand a gentle squeeze. "I know what you mean. It's okay, you know. I'd rather be your friend than nothing at all."

The door opened, and a young aide maneuvered a dinner tray through the narrow space between the bed and the wall. Her eyes opened wide when she saw me standing there. "Oh," she said and settled the tray onto the table. "You'd better go, miss. Nurse Sims is coming and you're not suppose to be here. She'll be awfully mad."

"I'll be back." I smiled at Sam. "I'll bring you a shake," I whispered when the aide turned her back. "A big, thick, chocolate one from Louie's."

Aunt Rose was waiting in the hall. A grim-faced older lady in a nurse uniform marched out of the room next to Sam's. She peered at us over her spectacles and frowned. Aunt Rose smiled and called, "Good day," and we caught the elevator just as the doors started to close.

* * *

No one could believe it, but Sam made it to graduation.

Neither of us was fit to go to the prom, but Dotty assured me it was boring anyway: "What can you expect when the school's two best dancers aren't there?"

I laughed and knotted the thread on my needle. "You know, I had to take this hem up five inches." I finished the last few slip stitches and shook out my graduation gown. It was purple with gold braid, for our school colors, and I knew I would wear it proudly even though I didn't like the color purple.

"Have you heard from Jake?"

I could hear the concern behind her smile. I had written him about what happened to me and Sam, but Jake hadn't answered my letter. I hoped it was because he was out to sea, maybe on his way home like he'd promised.

"Not yet," I said, hanging the gown on the door of my closet. We went downstairs and made cocoa to go with the plate of gingersnaps Aunt Rose had left out. But a gloom had settled over the day.

Later that night, after I'd already brushed my teeth and said good-night to the family, the phone rang.

"What on earth? Who could be calling this time of night?" I heard Aunt Rose's slippers scuff along the carpet in the hall.

"Stay put, Rose, I'll get it." Uncle Edward caught the phone on the fourth ring.

"Cissy," he called up the stairs, "it's for you."

My heart thumped and I flew to the phone. I mouthed the word *Jake* but Uncle Edward shook his head no.

It turned out to be Jake's brother Tim. "Jake said to call and tell you he should be home in time for graduation." His voice was so low I could hardly hear. "But," Tim went on, "he has to stop by here first. Maybe I'll come with him. Would you like that? Oh, heck, here comes Ma. Talk to you later, Cissy. Bye."

The line went dead before I could think to ask Tim any questions. But my mind churned. *Why didn't Jake just write— or call me himself?* I wondered if he was mad about Sam, or afraid of the men who had tried to run us over. He didn't know they'd been caught and put in jail. But no, I decided, that's not like Jake. He's not afraid of anything.

"He'll be here, sweetheart, don't worry so." Aunt Rose tried to soothe me, but by graduation day I was in such a stew I could hardly button the new dress I'd made to wear under my gown. It was a soft, white sleeveless crepe that floated just below my knees and fit like a dream. Jake would like it. If he ever got home.

Mama loved it. Uncle Edward had picked her up at noon, and she sat on the sofa waiting for me to come down. "Ah, my beautiful girl," she crooned when she saw the dress, "Papa would say you look like an angel and he'd be right."

I hugged her and she kissed my cheek. "I'm proud of you, darling. So are Papa and Krista, and the babies, even though they can't be here to tell you so."

I didn't remind her that "the babies" would be ten and almost six by now.

Aunt Rose called us in for supper before we could both tear up.

"Homemade soup and grilled cheese sandwiches!" Billy was at the table before anyone and had taken two bites of his sandwich before Uncle Edward said grace.

"Lord, we thank thee for Cissy," he prayed, "for allowing us to have her with our family. And we thank thee that Lynetta could be here to share her daughter's triumph . . ."

I felt a glow of happiness and added my own prayer of thanksgiving for my family. But I couldn't help the anxious feelings that gnawed at my stomach and made me push away my food.

"Don't be a nervous nelly," Mary Margaret chided. "Graduation is a cinch. Just wait until your wedding day. That's the killer."

Aunt Rose coughed, and Billy looked down at his plate. I smiled to show them I was fine, but my heart ached so bad I couldn't speak. Where was Jake? If he was coming, surely he'd be here by now.

Chapter
Twelve

Jake wasn't waiting at the stadium for the graduation cere-
monies, but Sam was—wheelchair and all. Everyone gave him
a standing ovation. Even Mama stood and clapped when he got
his diploma and again when they handed me mine. "I feel like
I know your friends, Celia," she told me. "Your letters are so
full of life."

That was the first time I knew she even read my letters, let
alone understood them. I decided that Mama's being there was
the best part of the ceremony.

I'd gone from worried to mad about Jake not coming. How
could he not show up when he'd promised? Tim wasn't there
either, so maybe Jake didn't get home, but he could have let me
know. When Sam insisted he was going to the party at the
Palace, I said I'd be proud to be his date.

Dotty came alone. The boy she'd been seeing had the flu.
Anyway, he was a year younger, still a junior, and she was
thinking of breaking up with him. She sat with Sam and me
and Bubbles Brannigan at a table for four and drank her punch
out of a champagne glass. She hovered around Sam all evening
and fussed over me like a mother hen. I knew she was only
trying to make me forget about Jake so I'd have a good time,

but enough was enough.

"I'm fine," I whispered when we went into the ladies' lounge. The room was as packed as the dance floor; girls stood around in clusters giggling and painting on fresh lipstick. "You don't have to treat me like I'm going to dry up and become an old maid. Why don't you find someone to dance with? This is your party too."

Her eyes lit up. "You're a swell friend, Cissy. I know just the one."

She raced back to the table and, before I could blink, grabbed the back of Sam's chair and wheeled him out onto the dance floor. The band was playing a red-hot version of "Tiger Rag," and I'll be switched if she and Sam didn't pick up the rhythm and jitterbug, chair and all.

They had the whole place almost rolling on the floor. I was wiping my eyes with the corner of my napkin, trying to stop laughing, when Bubbles' head snapped around and her mouth dropped open.

"Oh my, will you look at that. Quick, Cissy, how do I look? He's headed this way."

The music stopped, and I heard the brake on Sam's chair click shut next to me. I felt Dotty touch my arm and heard her whisper, "Good luck, honey." But my eyes were fixed on Jake as he handed the waiter a bill and wound his way through the throng of laughing, swaying bodies. He was wearing civvies: a clean white shirt, with the sleeves rolled up over his forearms, and a black silk tie.

He was, by far, the handsomest man I'd ever known.

We were alone in the room. He took my hand without a word, pulled me to my feet and out onto the dance floor. The band eased into "Sentimental Reasons." I closed my eyes and let the soft-sweet notes carry me away. Another couple bumped my arm as they whirled by, but Jake held me closer and laid his cheek against my hair.

We stayed just long enough for Jake to say hello to Dotty and for me to introduce him to the others. Bubbles gushed and giggled and spilled punch all down her dress when Jake said "Hi." He and Sam shook hands, and I thought Jake held on just a little too long.

I don't know what Sam was thinking. He nodded when Jake said, "I'm glad to meet you." But his smile was wistful and a little sad.

* * *

Jake had hitched a ride to Uncle Edward's and borrowed the car. We pulled into the driveway, and he shut off the engine but didn't make a move to open the door. Instead, he put his arm along the seat back and curled his hand around my shoulder. I shivered and closed my eyes, remembering the feel of his arms around me as we danced.

"Shouldn't we go in?" I really didn't want to, but I hated the thought of being in the driveway and having Aunt Rose come out to call the cat.

"Shh. Not yet. They know we're here. Your uncle and I had a talk."

I turned so I could look at him. I knew he could read the questions in my eyes, but he just stared at me like he wanted to memorize every freckle on my face. "I almost lost you," he choked. "Do you realize that, Cissy? I almost lost you forever, and I could never live with that."

"But you didn't, Jake. I'm here and I'll always be, I promise."

He lifted my left hand and kissed it. Then we both looked down and watched him slide a ring onto my finger. A tiny diamond in a shiny gold band. "Marry me, Cissy? Please say yes."

It was my turn not to answer. I threw my arms around his neck and kissed him instead.

* * *

The next few days were hectic as we made our plans. Jake only had a two-week leave, but he wanted to get things settled with his folks and decide on a place for us to live. "He'll be home for thirty days in January," I told Dotty as we pored over catalogs and magazines looking for ideas for my wedding dress. "We'll get married then and have a nice long honeymoon before he has to go back out to sea."

"Wahoo," she whistled, and I felt my face go red. Then I realized that she was pointing to a picture in the *Ladies Home Journal.* "Here's your dress, and mine too, here on page fourteen."

She was right. The gown was perfect and didn't look too hard to make.

Aunt Rose agreed, "It's beautiful, Cissy, but I'm not sure—"

"Don't worry, Aunt Rose. We have time. I can save my money and buy the material myself."

"And I'll pay for my own," Dotty volunteered.

Mrs. Garret, our typing teacher, had helped us land jobs in the typing pool at City Hall. "It should only take a week or two of evenings to make my dress. I can start cutting the pattern now and won't have to buy material till December."

Aunt Rose's face brightened. "I'll cut the patterns. You girls will be too busy. Let's see, we'll need to think about the flowers. Oh, dear, January isn't the best month, but we'll make do. I'm sure your mother will want to help, Cissy. Oh, grief! Have you told her yet?"

"Not yet." I had to pinch myself to keep from laughing. I'd never seen Aunt Rose in such a dither. "Jake and I thought we'd go over to the manor on Saturday." Mama had been moved to Havenwood Manor, a state-run sanatorium in Pasadena, only a few blocks from St. Stephen's Orphanage where I'd lived for a while.

"What about Sam?" Dotty creased the pages in the magazine to mark our spot and laid it on the kitchen table.

"What about him?"

"You haven't told him, have you? About you and Jake getting engaged." She was drawing circles on the table with her finger, but she held her body still and quiet as if waiting for the answer to some momentous question.

"I thought we'd tell him tonight at Donna's party."

I watched her face relax, and suddenly I knew. *Why, Dotty is in love with Sam! I never thought.* I started to ask her about it, then decided to hold my peace. How it must have hurt her to watch Sam dote over me when she knew my heart belonged to Jake. Now Sam would be free to find another girl—her, she hoped. And I hoped with all my heart that he would see it that way.

*   *   *

I felt strange and more than a little nervous walking into Donna's party that night. I grasped Jake's hand. He flinched but squeezed mine back and whispered, "Relax, babe, it's okay."

As the party went on, it was hard to forget the last time I was here. Hard not to close my eyes and hear an engine roar and the thump of steel hitting a body. I could almost feel the blood in my eyes and the fear when Sam didn't call out or move.

Stop it.

I took a long swallow from my glass and gasped. How Donna had convinced her mother to let her serve champagne I'd never know.

Mary Lou was standing beside me in the kitchen doorway. "This stuff is horrible." I bent my head and whispered so Donna wouldn't hear.

"Oh, I don't know. It's not so bad," she grinned. "In fact, I kind of like it."

I handed her my glass and pushed my way into the kitchen

to get some water. Several people stopped me to admire my ring. When I made it back into the living room, I saw Jake and Sam over by the fireplace. Jake was on his haunches, both hands on the wheelchair, looking into Sam's face. They both looked so serious, and Sam was watching Jake closely, intent on what he had to say.

Dotty had propped herself against the fireplace only a few inches behind Sam's chair. I started toward them, but she motioned me to stop and came to me instead. There were tears in her eyes as she grabbed my arm and led me toward Donna's bedroom.

"Do you know what a prize you have?" She sobbed when she had shut the door.

"Yes," I sputtered when she threw her arms around my neck and blubbered all over my good lace collar. "But what on earth are you bawling about?" I moved her back a ways. "Whew. You've been drinking Donna's champagne."

"So what?" She let me loose and folded herself onto Donna's bed. "Jake is out there pledging his life to Sam because of what he did for you." She sniffed, "Going on and on about how grateful he is and how Sam should know he'd do anything to help if he needs it."

I fished a hankie from my beaded bag and handed it to her. I'd never known Jake to let his feelings show the way Dotty described it, but I had no doubt she was telling the truth. Jake had never been jealous of Sam. In fact, I think he was glad I had someone to go out with. A friend to take care of me when he wasn't there.

According to Dotty, that's just what he'd been telling Sam. "He thanked him for taking care of you, and asked if he was up to it for another few months. And you know what he said, Cissy? You know what Sam said?"

I shook my head, but she had leaned down to examine a run

in one of the new nylon stockings she'd gotten for graduation.

"He said," she sniffed and wiped her eyes, " 'As long as Dotty's willing to help me.' You hear that, Cissy?" She looked at me and I could see the joy well up. "He wants me to help him. Sam *wants* me."

Chapter
Thirteen

There were no bars on the windows at Havenwood Manor. The grounds were as well kept as those at the hospital, but that's where the resemblance ended. The rest of the place was clean and neat, with white painted walls and bright red carpets. The scent from fresh-cut flowers wafted through the reception room, and open windows let in clean air.

Mama was on the patio, seated in a white wicker chair next to a small glass-top table. She had a shredded piece of quilt spread across her knees and was gazing contentedly out across the grounds.

"Look who's here, Mama. I've brought Jake along."

She nodded her head regally and allowed us both to kiss her cheek.

"We have something to tell you, Mama." I took a deep breath. "Jake and I want to get married."

She smiled her secret smile, and it was impossible to tell if she was listening or not. I prodded Jake, and he leaned over to where she had to look at him.

"Mrs. Summers? I love your daughter, and I'd like your permission to marry her."

Her smile brightened. "Jake Freeman, you always were a

scamp. Have you talked to Charles?"

Jake stood up and looked at me. I fought the urge to shake her shoulders. She'd seemed fine at graduation. Why'd she have to go back to her dream world now?

I knelt down by her chair. "Papa isn't here," I said as gently as I could. "Jake talked to Uncle Edward. He's given us permission."

It was true. Aunt Rose and Uncle Edward had both approved our plans, but not without some hesitancy. I knew they were concerned because Jake didn't go to church very often. Jake told me they'd had a long talk the night of graduation before he came to get me at the Palace. When I asked him what they talked about, he just grinned. "The world, the flesh and the devil," was all he'd say.

Mama's head snapped up when I mentioned Uncle Edward. "Oh, dear, I'm afraid Charles and Edward don't get along." Then she brightened. "Well, we just won't tell Charles my brother's involved. I'm sure he'd want you to be happy."

Suddenly she stood, straightened her skirt and tucked a lock of snow-white hair back behind her ear. Jake retrieved the quilt piece she'd dropped from her lap, along with a needle and spool of thread I hadn't noticed before. He tried to hand it back to her, but she had already turned and was leaning on the railing that surrounded the patio like a porch. He gave it over to me instead, and I recognized it right away.

This is Krista's quilt. What's left of it anyway. Mama had been mending it. Or trying to. The stitches were odd and uneven, more like a four-year-old's first efforts than the quality stitching I remembered. She had made this quilt with scraps from some of Grandma Eva's old dresses.

I closed my eyes. I could see her, sitting on the wide front porch of our home in Pike, Nevada, arms propped across her bulging stomach, her fingers taking tiny stitches, pushing the needle through with Grandma's silver thimble. I was five and I'd been sitting at her feet, playing with the spools of brightly colored thread, stacking them like towers and toppling them over onto the clean-swept concrete.

Mama had stood up suddenly then too. She'd handed me the quilt and grabbed the porch railing so hard I could see her fingers turn pale. "Take this in the house," she groaned. Then she took a breath and her voice got stronger. "Take this in, Cissy, then run fetch Mrs. Wilson. Tell her the baby's coming. Do you understand?"

I nodded.

"Go then. Hurry."

She clutched her stomach again and I ran. Mrs. Wilson came, then the midwife. Before long I was sitting at Grandma Eva's kitchen table eating oatmeal cookies and drinking cocoa. When she took me back home that evening, Krista was lying next to Mama, all pink and pretty and smelling so sweet.

"Cissy?" I felt Jake's arm around my waist. "Should we go now, or what?"

Mama was still at the rail, her eyes sweeping the sky and grass, looking for . . . what? Then she turned, and the joy in her eyes was unmistakable. "Oh, I'm so happy. And Papa will be pleased. You two run along now," she shooed us with her hands. "I'm sure you have a lot to do. Why, I must find something to wear to the wedding. Do you suppose I can make something up in time?"

I laughed, and Jake looked relieved. "You've got time, Mama; the wedding isn't until January." I hugged her hard, and Jake kissed her on the cheek.

"We'll come back, Mrs. Summers."

"See you do." She smiled and took his hands. "And give my best to your mama."

* * *

It was almost a relief when Jake was gone and life settled back into a routine.

Except for the fact that Dotty and I sat at bigger desks, working at City Hall wasn't much different than school. We typed and took dictation from businessmen instead of teachers and got paychecks instead of report cards.

I gave some of my pay to Uncle Edward. "For rent," I insisted when he didn't want to take it. "You've done so much for me, and Mama too. Please, I want to start paying my own way." I knew the sanatorium was expensive, and without Uncle Edward Mama would be cooped up in a state institution.

He and Aunt Rose had tried to talk her into coming home with us, but she'd refused. "I won't be a burden to any of you. You've done enough by caring for Cissy." Uncle Edward had talked to a lawyer, and next thing I knew, she was settled at Havenwood and happier than I'd seen her in a long, long time.

Uncle Edward finally gave in and took fifty cents a month from my pay. The rest I spent on bus fare and household goods for my hope chest. Aunt Rose kept finding things to add. Even Mary Margaret brought some things from her apartment.

"You can have these towels, Cissy, and this platter too; it doesn't match the rest of my dishes."

Mary Margaret looked tired and drawn. She said she was fine and stayed busy keeping house and drinking tea with her landlady. But I knew she was bored and she seemed unhappy. Wesley was away most of the time. He'd been out to sea again, but he came home for a few days in October, and the next time I saw Mary Margaret she had a bruise the size of a half-dollar on her cheek.

"What happened?" I gasped.

"I bumped it on the cupboard door." She shrugged and went back to sorting beans to go with the hamhock Aunt Rose had saved for Sunday dinner.

* * *

The first Saturday in December, Dotty and I went shopping for material. The days that followed disappeared like pennies down a well. With Aunt Rose's help we had the dresses done by Christmas Eve.

Billy had found a Christmas tree and set it up all by himself. He fetched the decorations from the attic and made a wreath of cedar clippings for the front door.

Mary Margaret had shown up that morning with her travel case. "Wesley's ship docked in New York," she said, "and he can't get home for Christmas. But he promised he'd try and make it for the wedding."

She set her case down on the bed and spun around.

"Do you like my new dress? I made it myself."

I tried not to look surprised. Mary Margaret hadn't wanted a homemade dress in years. *She must really be bored.*

"Why, it's nice," I stammered. "You did a great job. I should have let you make my wedding dress!"

Her face glowed with my compliment.

Later, I found her in the kitchen stirring batter for a coffee-cake. She smiled as she worked and hummed "Silent Night." I took some plates down from the cupboard and began to set the table for supper. I couldn't help but hum along with her. Aunt Rose joined us, and in a few minutes we were singing the words in three-part harmony. "Sleep in heav-en-ly pe-eace, sle-eep in heav-en-ly peace."

Mary Margaret hugged us both and smiled.

Chapter
Fourteen

I decided I would change my name to Celia when I married Jake. Not legally, of course; there was no need for that. Celia was my given name, but I'd been called Cissy for so long most people had forgotten my real one. I don't think Jake even knew until the day we went to get our blood tests.

"Celia Marie Summers," I replied when the clerk asked for my full name.

Jake looked down at me, and then he snatched the birth certificate out of my hand. "What's this?" He chuckled and held it just out of my reach. "Are you telling me the girl I fell in love with is really someone else?"

I felt my face get hot and red, like Jake's when he was in a temper. But I wasn't mad, just embarrassed by his teasing.

"Jake Freeman! You give me that and stop your fooling. The man is waiting for those papers."

"Yes, ma'am!" Jake brought his hand up in a mock salute and pushed our birth certificates across the counter. Then he reached into the pocket of his navy blues, peeled off a brand-new dollar bill and handed it with ceremony to the clerk.

"There," he said as we reached the top of the courthouse steps, "that's done. Soon you'll be Mrs. Jake L. Freeman." He picked me up and whirled me around, and I had to curl my toes to keep my new white pumps from flying off my feet. "How do you like that, Cissy?" He set me on the ground and tugged on the veil of my sailor hat to straighten it. "I mean *Celia*, Celia Marie Freeman. It sounds like something a lark would sing."

"I like it fine, Jake," I whispered and let him kiss me right there in front of God and the entire city of Los Angeles.

* * *

He didn't kiss me again until the wedding. There wasn't time. His ship had been due in on the twenty-eighth. His father had agreed to pick him up in San Diego and bring him straight to San Bernardino to meet Pastor Stewart and learn his lines. As it turned out, the ship was three days late. Mr. Freeman couldn't get away, and Uncle Edward wound up driving down to San Diego on New Year's Eve.

"I'll take the bus," Jake hollered over the static on the phone. But Aunt Rose wouldn't hear of it.

"You'll have to go and get him, Edward. Pastor Stewart will be here at seven, and the party starts at eight. What a time for that blessed ship to be late. Well, that's the Navy for you. A day late and a dollar short every time!"

Uncle Edward laughed and pulled her closer for a hug. "Don't get yourself so riled up; you sound like my mother. This will all sort out, you'll see." He kissed her hair.

I smiled in spite of the fact that I was nervous too. Aunt Rose did sound like Grandma Eva when she was "vexed."

Grandma Eva never had much good to say about the Navy— or any branch of the service, for that matter. Her husband, my grandfather, had served a hitch during the Great War and come home without the middle finger on his left hand.

"He caught it between the gun-stock and the mount," Grandma explained, "and he was never the same again, in body or in spirit."

"When your grandpa came home, she blamed the Navy for every one of his faults," Mama had told me. "Even when he had a heart attack and died in the bathtub, she said, 'It's only fitting he should die in the water—he surely spent more time in it than he did with me.' "

"Are you going, sweetheart?" I jumped and realized Uncle Edward was talking to me.

I looked at Aunt Rose.

"Of course she's going!" She handed me my sweater and shooed me toward the door.

I hesitated. I really wanted to go with Uncle Edward. My pulse raced at the very thought of seeing Jake. The last three days had been an agony of waiting, and I didn't want to put off seeing him a minute longer. "But what about the party?"

The door opened, and Dotty popped her head in without knocking. "Is he here yet?" She handed Aunt Rose a tray of canapés, tiny squares of white bread filled with tuna salad and a sliver of green olive on top.

"There, you see? Dorothy's here to help me. Thank you, dear." She handed Dotty back the platter and pushed her toward the kitchen. "You go on now, Cissy. I mean *Celia.* Oh dear, I'll never get it right." She kissed Uncle Edward's cheek. "Go on now, both of you, or the party will start without the bride and groom."

* * *

We couldn't have wished for a nicer day. The sun peeked into the church through a stained-glass window and focused its beam on the altar, bathing it in a gentle glow that stayed there all through the ceremony. "Like God smiling at us," I told Aunt Rose later. She agreed he surely was.

It took a little while for the wedding to get started. The rings were tied with ribbon to a white satin pillow that Jake's little brother, Davy, was supposed to carry down the aisle. The music had already started when Davy threw the pillow to his big sister Anne and dashed down the stairs like he was being chased by a hornet.

Anne ran after him. The organist played another chorus of the "Wedding March" and they soon returned, Davy looking much relieved and Anne running along behind frantically trying to refasten his suspenders.

Amy, Davy's twin, dropped her flower basket halfway down the aisle and refused to budge a step farther until she had retrieved every petal. Mrs. Freeman looked mortified and kept trying to wave her on, but Amy was oblivious to anything but her precious flowers.

We were all a little nervous. I just knew I would take a misstep and trip on my gown, but I made it to the front. Jake looked relieved when we finally stood side by side.

Dotty's hands shook when she reached for my bouquet and handed me the ring: Papa's wedding band, which Jake had agreed to wear. Mama had given it to us the night of the party. "Papa would want you to have this, dear," she said and handed me a folded lace hankie with the ring inside. "It's our wedding present to you both."

I unfolded the cloth and held it out to Jake. *Will you wear it?* I had asked with my eyes. He had answered, *I'd be proud.*

"Do you take this woman . . ." The pastor asked us to repeat our vows.

". . . in sickness and in health . . ."

". . . till death do us part . . ."

The rings slid on. Jake and I joined hands and knelt before the altar. It was finished. One person. One body. Forever.

We ran back down the aisle and formed a reception line outside the church. Jake's brother Tim was the first in line to kiss me. Sam was second, but he kissed Dotty too, and when I threw my bouquet, Dotty moved in front of Mary Lou and made a clean catch. Sam held it on his lap, and they were laughing as Dotty wheeled him away.

* * *

Mr. Freeman gave us train fare, and we went to San Diego for our honeymoon.

Our hotel room was small, with an old-fashioned flower carpet that looked a hundred years old. The bed was barely big enough for two. Jake said, "Never mind. We don't need a bigger bed," and wiggled his eyebrows just like Groucho Marx.

We only had five days in San Diego, but they were filled with laughter and enough love to coat the world in a bright rosy glow.

We took the bus down to the waterfront. I admired Jake's ship—"my home away from home," he called it—and met a couple of his friends. But when they asked us to a party, Jake said no. "I don't want to share you with anyone," he told me.

We bought some cotton candy that melted into sweet pink sugar on our tongues. We inhaled the damp salt air, explored stuffy little curio shops and took a chance on a "fresh-caught oyster, guaranteed to hold a pearl."

We built a bonfire on the beach, roasted hot dogs dipped in mustard and ate them sand and all. Then, on the night before we had to catch the train back home, we ran barefoot down Main Street at midnight in the pouring rain and almost got arrested for being drunk and disorderly. Jake assured the policeman we were "just drunk on love." He must have sounded convincing, because the patrolman let us go without checking Jake's ID.

"Whew, that was close," Jake whispered as we walked hand in hand through the hotel lobby. "If they had called the SPs we would have been in for it."

By the time the train pulled into the station and Uncle Edward helped Jake get our bags to the car, Jake and I were both sneezing and shaking with chills.

"Jake says I can live on base," I told Aunt Rose a few days later. "The apartments are small, but that's just less to keep clean."

She handed me a cup of tea and a tissue for my dripping nose. "I won't hear of it!" She glared at Jake like he was related to the Devil. "I'll not have you by yourself at some rat-infested Navy base! Tell them, Edward. She must stay right here with us, at least until Jake comes home."

"She's right, Celia." Uncle Edward put his arm around my shoulders. "This is your home for as long as you want to stay."

Their kindness made me feel warm and loved.

Jake shook Uncle Edward's hand. "Thank you, sir. I'll feel better knowing she's safe here with you."

"I'm glad I'll be staying here awhile," I told Dotty later. "I sure didn't want to live with strangers."

Dotty nodded, "Once you've been married, it must be awful to have to live anywhere without your husband."

I felt my face flush red. Did Jake know how good it felt to belong to him? I longed for the day when he'd be out of the Navy and we could be together forever.

* * *

"Tell me again when you'll be home to stay."

Jake propped himself up on his elbow and traced a finger across my eyes. He drew it along the side of my nose and laid it gently against my lips.

"Shh. I told you, babe, Only a few months. I'll be out in July. We'll be settled in our own place by Christmas."

"Then what, Jake? What will you do?"

He wadded up his pillow and stuffed it back under his head. "I want to fly, Celia. That's all I've ever wanted to do."

I felt uneasy for the first time since Jake proposed. Oh, we'd talked about it all before. How he wanted to be a pilot. I'd heard almost a year ago that some planes were carrying passengers now. Maybe Jake could fly people around the country. When I had mentioned it, he shook his head. "How could I ever afford the schooling? Besides, it's not the same as flying for your country."

That was when he believed he'd be assigned to a carrier and somehow learn to fly. But even though he'd been promoted to Fireman First Class, he was still a machinist's mate, stuck in the belly of whatever ship they assigned him to.

"But how? If you get out of the Navy . . ."

He squeezed my hand. "I'll find a way. If it's the last thing I do, I'll find a way."

* * *

Jake went back to San Diego February 1, and Sam and Dotty moved to Los Angeles.

Sam had enrolled at UCLA for the winter term. He was still in a wheelchair, but he was determined to get his law degree.

"I want to put men like the ones who did this in prison," he said, slapping the armrest on his chair, "and see to it that they stay there."

Sam wasn't really bitter about his injuries, just determined to overcome them and get on with his life. He was getting impatient, though. The doctors still sidestepped the big question: "Will this be permanent?" Sam repeated it every time they drew blood or took an x-ray, but they would just say, "It's too early to tell," and send him on his way until the next round of tests.

Jake and I both tried to avoid talking about the gangsters who had almost killed Sam. "It's over, babe," he said when I brought it up one day. "Those creeps are locked up for good."

"What about parole, Jake? What if they come after you next time?"

"Let 'em try," he growled. "Just let 'em try."

Now Jake was gone and Dotty too. She'd found a job and an apartment in the same building as Sam's. She was taking a business class at the university, but I knew that was just an excuse to be near him.

"I'll be there to see he eats right and takes his medicine," she told me as she helped him into the car. She kissed his cheek and Sam rolled his eyes.

"What am I going to do, Celia? She'll nag me to death before she's through." He flicked a gum wrapper in Dotty's direction, but I could see gratitude in his eyes, and a growing affection that I hoped would turn to love.

Chapter
Fifteen

Somehow I knew Jake would not be home in July. It was written between the lines in every letter I received from March through May. They all began, "My Darling Girl," and ended, "My Love Always, Jake," but in between were lines that read: "I'm up for promotion in June," "I get extra pay for being married. How about that, babe?" "They just put up new housing at the aviation training base in Pensacola."

It was obvious he wanted to reenlist. "It scares me," I told Dotty during one of our monthly phone calls. "With everything that's happening in Europe . . . What if we get involved?" I tried to keep the anxiety out of my replies to Jake. I said, "I miss you," and "I can't wait to be with you again," but I tried not to complain.

Wesley ranted and raved at Mary Margaret, saying she made his life miserable when he was out to sea.

"What happened, Celia? Wesley used to say I was the most beautiful girl in the world and that he couldn't stand to be away from me. Now he calls me awful names and doesn't want to come home at all."

I could only hug her and listen to her fears. It wouldn't help to tell her things would get better, because I felt sure that wasn't true. Wesley Harris was a restless man with an eye for the ladies. He'd had Mary Margaret on a string since high school, but we all knew he was seeing other girls as well. "That will change when we get married!" she had said so confidently. Now I didn't have the heart to say "I told you so." Mary Margaret was so fragile now, I was afraid any extra hurt would destroy her.

We were sitting on the sofa one Saturday morning in June when Mary Margaret was visiting, trying to decide if we would see a show or watch Billy's baseball game at the park.

"Mail's here." Billy came through the screen door, a catcher's mitt dangling from one hand and a stack of letters in the other.

"Sorry, sis, none for you. Cissy, I mean *Celia*, you got one from Dotty and one from Jake!" He dangled Jake's letter just out of reach. "Let's see," he held the envelope at arm's length up to the light. "It says, 'My darling dearest sweetest flame . . .' "

"William." Aunt Rose set a vase of sweet peas on the end table. "Don't be such a pest. Give Cissy her letter."

Aunt Rose still called me Cissy. The others tried to remember, but, as Mama always said, old habits die hard, and I told them I really didn't mind. Mary Margaret had no trouble at all. "I'm glad you've gone back to your real name," she'd said. "You're a married woman now, not a baby anymore."

I almost opened Dotty's letter first. I was always excited to hear from Jake, but I felt uneasy about this letter. Maybe because the time was getting short and I knew Jake had not yet realized his dream.

It turned out I was right.

"There is a chance, babe. A slight one, but a chance. Lieutenant Donnor said he'd put in a word for me with the commander. If I re-up it could mean another promotion and a shot at becoming a pilot. Besides, how will I support you if I get out? I don't want to be a mechanic all my life, and we can't afford for me to go to college. I want the best for us, Celia, and sometimes the best comes with a price."

He went on to say he missed me, "but I'll be home at Christmas time for sure. I've been transferred to a battleship. Can you believe that? The USS *West Virginia.* We're supposed to dock at Pearl sometime in December. How would you like to live in Hawaii? Not a bad deal, huh, babe?"

"At least he's coming home for a while," I sighed and showed the letter to Mary Margaret. "And they can't send him overseas if he's in training. Can they?"

She shrugged. "The Navy can do anything it wants to, Celia. Take it from me, as long as Jake is in the service he might as well be married to it."

The war in Europe was in full swing, and we both knew either Wesley or Jake might have to go if it didn't end soon. I had decided not to read the paper while Jake was gone. But that lasted less than a week. Besides, Uncle Edward or Billy always had the radio on and I couldn't help hearing the news.

Germany and "that maniac," as Uncle Edward called Hitler, had been devouring countries since 1938. Now German U-boats in the Atlantic were venturing closer to America and the U.S. Navy was threatening to attack.

We were all a little nervous.

* * *

December 7, 1941. We didn't go to church that morning. Aunt Rose had gone to bed the night before with one of her migraine headaches, and we were all tired.

I did up the breakfast dishes and hung my apron on the hook in the broom closet. I planned to spend the morning sorting through drawers and wrapping Christmas presents, but Uncle Edward got out the Bible and called Billy and me into the living room.

"If we can't attend service," he said, "we can at least have family devotions."

Billy ducked his head but folded himself into a sitting position on the floor. His undershirt hung loose across his skinny chest, and his ears stuck out from a mop of unruly black hair. At fifteen, Billy still had some filling out to do.

He was smart, our Billy, but stubborn, and the only thing he really liked to study was baseball. He dreamed of being a star pitcher someday, and Uncle Edward had a hard time convincing him that school had to come first.

Uncle Edward perched on the corner of the sofa and opened his Bible. His face glowed, like it always did when he read Scripture. You could tell he believed every word. By the time he finished thanking God for our family and asking him to bless the president and our nation, my mind had drifted to thoughts of Jake. Aunt Rose moaned softly from the bedroom. Uncle Edward said, "Amen," and rushed in to her, leaving Billy and me to our own devices.

I went off to my room—soon to be mine and Jake's. Mary Margaret had been gone two years, and I'd had no trouble taking over the entire closet and dresser. Jake had left some of his civvies here after our honeymoon. I had my work cut out getting ready for him to come home.

I moved a stack of sweaters from one drawer to another, then tugged on the sheet of Mary Margaret's wedding paper that lined the drawer. It wouldn't give, so I ran my hand underneath to loosen the tape. My fingers brushed against a piece of paper stuck in the crack at the back of the drawer. I pulled it out and smiled as I opened the folded note carefully.

"Don't worry, Cissy. Everything will be all right. Love, Jake."

I sat down on the bed and held the paper to my cheek. Jake. It was the first note he'd ever written me. On my fourteenth birthday—the day that Papa died.

I felt a twinge of fear, then brushed it away. *That's over, Celia,* I told myself, *over and done. You're a grown woman. Jake's your husband and he's coming home soon!*

My husband! It sounded strange even to my own ears. We'd been married such a short time before he'd gone back out to sea. Those thirty days of liberty had sounded like a long time to get our marriage started, but they'd gone by like a leaf in a puff of wind.

Another thirty days and he would be gone again. But this time I was going with him. *Why should it matter so much that I don't know where?*

I heard Uncle Edward whistling as he raked twigs from under the apple tree. In the living room, Billy snapped on the radio. I smiled, content with my task and the background sounds of family life.

I'll miss them when Jake and I move out.

The telephone interrupted my thoughts. I rushed into the living room, motioning for Billy to turn down the radio. He grinned and turned the volume knob. Everyone knew I was waiting to hear from Jake. His ship was due in Hawaii any day, and he'd promised to call as soon as he could get away. He'd be home for Christmas, we were sure of it.

* * *

Once in a while time rolls by in slow motion. Like an old Victrola winding down. I can see the telephone clearly, a big black box with a rotary dial. The numbers on white cardboard seemed to jump out at me as I snatched up the receiver.

I can still taste the disappointment when I realized it was only Dotty. She says I wasn't rude, but to this day I don't remember our conversation.

I remember hanging up, though. And Billy turning up the radio. Uncle Edward walked into the room, dusting off his work pants.

"Dad," Billy's words sounded shaky, "where is Pearl Harbor?"

Uncle Edward looked annoyed. "If you had paid attention in your geography classes . . ." He stopped when he saw Billy's face. I couldn't drag my eyes away from him either. His skin was a sickly gray.

Uncle Edward stood stock still. "Why?"

"Because we've just been bombed." Billy whispered. "Wherever it is, we've just been bombed there."

A beam of sunlight filtered through the window behind Aunt Rose's just-washed sheers. I knew Pearl Harbor. Even though I'd never been there, I knew it from Jake's letters.

The room faded in and out like the pictures in a slide show. Someone screamed and kept on screaming. I clenched my fists and pressed them against my ears to stop the noise. It wasn't until Uncle Edward picked me up and carried me to the sofa that I realized the screams were pouring out of my own throat.

* * *

I awoke to cool darkness. At first I thought I was back at St. Stephen's Orphanage in my closet room. Sister Anne would come soon to collect me for morning chores.

When I turned my head, a damp cloth slipped from my eyes. I snatched it away and sat up in bed.

Jake!

Mary Margaret groaned as she turned over in the other bed. Memories of the day before came rushing back. I felt a knot of pain form at the base of my neck and spread to my head and face. If yesterday was real, Jake could very well be dead.

Mary Margaret moaned again and flipped her covers to the floor. We'd heard the news about the bombing around eleven yesterday morning, and Wesley had brought her over in a taxi around four in the afternoon. He'd been wearing his dress blues, the silver ensign bar gleaming on his collar and a matching gleam of excitement in his dark eyes.

Mary Margaret was in tears, of course. Wesley practically shoved her in the door, slapped Uncle Edward on the arm and headed back to the taxi. "Take care of her for me, will you, Pops? I got a ship to catch!"

Mary Margaret cried even harder. "He didn't even kiss me good-by!" she wailed.

At least you know for sure he's alive! I wanted to scream at her. My heart felt like someone had ripped it from my chest. I was fourteen again, huddled in a corner of the closet, stunned and grieving over Papa's death.

Krista, Mama, Chuckie, Grace. All the losses from my childhood seemed to pile up in front of me like a stack of unwashed laundry, until I could see nothing but the heartache.

Chapter
Sixteen

The clock in the living room chimed nine o'clock. I dragged myself out of bed and down to the kitchen for a glass of juice. Mama always swore a glass of orange juice and a good cry would cure a headache. I'd certainly had my fill of tears. My mouth tasted like the inside of an old galosh.

At least the juice will help that.

I grabbed two oranges from the basket on the counter and dug the squeezer out of the utensil drawer.

"Oh, good. Make me some too, Celia. My head is throbbing."

Mary Margaret plopped herself down at the kitchen table and rubbed her eyes with both fists. She looked like she'd been in the ring with Joe Louis. The image almost made me smile, but Wesley's face replaced Joe's and it wasn't funny anymore. Anyway, I probably looked just as bad.

"I want a hot bath, too," she muttered, "and coffee. Is there any coffee?" She crossed her arms on the red chrome table and lowered her head like a distraught child. "Cissy, what are we going to do?"

My heart went out to her in spite of my own pain. She hadn't known a minute's peace since the day she married Wesley, and she didn't even understand why.

Around ten, Uncle Edward went next door to see if Captain Long could help us get more information about the attack. He was back before I finished my juice.

"He doesn't know any more than we do." Uncle Edward hung his jacket on the hook inside the entry closet door. "He was in a hurry to get back to his old base. All he said was, 'I'm gonna show them young beggars how to fight a war!' "

"I bet he will," Billy mumbled. He'd been glued to the radio since Sunday's announcement about the bombing. For all I knew he'd been there all night. His T-shirt and jeans were the same ones he'd been wearing the day before, only a little more rumpled. His hair looked wild too, but his face stayed calm as he absorbed every word about the disaster.

William Shirer, Pierre Huss, Edward R. Murrow and Bob Trout told the thing over and over until I thought my head would burst. But they never told which ships had gone down, only that there had been hundreds of casualties.

Aunt Rose finally sent Billy in to wash and change. He was back in under five minutes with his hair slicked back, wearing a clean shirt.

None of us had the energy to move very far, so we were all in the living room when Mr. Roosevelt addressed the nation.

"Yesterday, December 7, 1941, a day which will live in infamy, the United States of America was suddenly and deliberately attacked by naval and air forces of the empire of Japan."

America was at war.

*　*　*

I recognized Tom Keltso's battered Model-T the minute it pulled in the drive.

"A telegram."

Mary Margaret stared at me, and Aunt Rose jumped to her feet.

"Sit still, I'll get it," Uncle Edward said, waving us all back to our seats.

I couldn't move. Maybe it was from Jake, telling me he was safe and would see me tomorrow. Or maybe it was from the War Department telling me he was dead. I tore open the envelope, then changed my mind and handed it to Uncle Edward. He unfolded the small white sheet of paper and read the few short lines:

> Arrived Pearl Harbor yesterday STOP Will call soon STOP I love you STOP Jake.

It was dated December 6, one day before the disaster.

We all went to bed early that night. Even Uncle Edward's face showed the strain of the last two days. He'd stayed home from work. He went to a prayer meeting at church, but was home by 7:30.

Billy stayed quiet, like he'd been since the bombing, but he ate two bowls of soup and a cheese sandwich for dinner and Aunt Rose looked relieved. I couldn't seem to swallow a thing.

Billy cleared his own plate and kissed Aunt Rose good-night. Then he came around the table and kissed Mary Margaret on the cheek. She looked surprised, but didn't say anything. When he stopped behind his father's chair, I thought he would kiss Uncle Edward too, but he moved on to me and I could read the misery in his eyes as he bent to kiss me on the forehead.

I gave him the "What's up?" look that we'd used on each other since he was ten, but he turned his head away, scooped up Tarzan and carried him off to his room.

"An early night will do us all good," Uncle Edward said and pushed away from the table. "You ladies can do dishes in the morning."

* * *

When we woke up the next morning, we found Tarzan licking the dried soup off the bowls on the kitchen table. It wasn't until we had cleaned the kitchen and done the rest of the morning chores that we realized Billy was gone.

Uncle Edward found the note pinned to his bedspread. The room was clean, the bed made up, and his clothes folded neatly in the drawers. As near as we could tell, he'd taken only some socks and one change of underwear.

"Dear Mom and Dad, please don't be mad. Someone has to get those Japs. I love you all, Billy."

"He's gone to war!" Mary Margaret screeched and crumpled onto Billy's bed.

Aunt Rose burst into tears. "Edward, you have to do something. That boy is much too young be on his own."

I felt numb. First Jake, now Billy too. When would this nightmare end?

* * *

A few hours later, the airwaves crackled as news from Pearl Harbor trickled in. The USS *Arizona* was a total loss. Jake's ship, the *West Virginia*, sat half submerged on the bottom of the Pacific Ocean. There had been some survivors, but no names were released.

At the latest report, there are over 400 dead and hundreds missing. Many of the injured are being treated at the naval hospital at Pearl, while others have been taken to emergency centers in Oahu.

The remainder of the fleet moved back out to sea last night. Meanwhile the blackout continues as all of Hawaii is under a state of emergency, and military censorship has been applied to all outgoing communication.

Uncle Edward tried to contact the Red Cross, but he couldn't get through.

"There's nothing more we can do, girls." He put his arm around Aunt Rose and squeezed my hand. "We'll find out soon, sweetheart. Jake's a fighter. Chances are he's in a cozy bed sleeping off some bumps and bruises."

I nodded, and bowed my head when he began to pray, but I didn't believe it. "What do you want, God? What do you want me to do?" My soul cried out its own prayer, and the answer came quiet and true: "Just trust."

I wasn't sure I could.

Chapter Seventeen

It had been five days since the attack on Pearl—four since our Billy took off. Uncle Edward had gone back to work. Aunt Rose was pale, but determined to stay busy. She had Mary Margaret helping her iron sheets with the mangle.

My mind was numb, and my eyes ached from too many tears and too little sleep. I had just rung out a rag in vinegar water to wipe a thumbprint from the window glass, when Tom Keltso's Model-T rattled up the driveway and Tom stepped out onto the grass.

When I saw the smile on his face, I ran to the door. My hands shook so bad I dropped the telegram twice before I could get it open.

I read the words and almost fainted with relief.

Everything's okay STOP Lester Drain

"Who's Lester Drain?" Mary Margaret read the telegram and handed it to Aunt Rose.

"I don't know," I stammered and slumped down in the wing-back chair. "But he must know Jake. Why else would he send this to me?" It crossed my mind then that it might be a mistake.

What if the message was from a friend of Billy's? I could tell Aunt Rose thought it might be.

It has to be about Jake. It has to.

Aunt Rose and Mary Margaret studied the telegram like it would change into a letter any minute and tell us everything we wanted to know.

* * *

A letter finally came the next day. But from Billy, not Jake.

Dear Mom and Dad,

Boy, am I tired. They're marching our legs off! I have blisters on top of blisters, but we're working extra hard so we can get out of here and go after them Japs.

I have to be up at 5:00 A.M. so I'd better get some shut-eye. Just wanted you to know I'm fine, except for a sore arm where they gave me some shots. You shoulda seen that needle!

I'll send you an address when I get one. Tell Celia and Sis hi for me.

Your loving son, Billy

"It doesn't say much, does it?" Mary Margaret handed the single sheet of paper back to her mother.

"At least we know he's all right." Aunt Rose dabbed her eyes and went to the phone to call Uncle Edward.

I felt relieved to know Billy was safe. But every day that passed without news of Jake left me more fearful than the day before. I tried to pray but couldn't get past "Please, God, just bring him home."

Uncle Edward read the letter and hugged Aunt Rose. "Billy's fine, you see? He's doing his part for his country. God will take care of him for us."

Aunt Rose went white and still as stone. I could tell her eyes saw nothing but Uncle Edward's face. "What do you mean he's doing his part? He's only fifteen, Edward. He had to lie about his age or they wouldn't have let him join. You have to put a stop to this nonsense and get him home now!"

Uncle Edward's smile faded and his shoulders drooped. "I can't make him come home, Rose, don't you see?" He looked right past us out the window like he was somewhere else. "I'd go myself, but they won't take me. 'Too old,' they said. Can you imagine? I'm too old to serve my country."

Aunt Rose went even whiter, and I helped her to the sofa. Uncle Edward came back from wherever his mind had wandered and sat beside her. "We have to let him go, Rosie," he said gently. "We have to let the boy grow up. Don't you see? If we forced him to come home, we'd lose him just as surely as if he'd gone to war."

They never talked about it after that. They laughed and cried together when we got his letters, and Aunt Rose baked him cookies and we all wrote almost every day. But never again did anyone suggest that Billy should come home.

*　*　*

Mary Margaret heard from Wesley the next day. He telephoned to say he was leaving that evening for an unknown destination. Mary Margaret pouted and said he should be able to tell his own wife where he was going and when he was coming back. He told her to quit acting like a spoiled kid and he'd see her when he saw her.

"He sounded more excited about going to war than sad about leaving me," she told me later.

I remembered how Aunt Rose and Uncle Edward had warned her not to marry Wesley. "He's too unsettled, honey," Aunt Rose had reasoned. "Sailors usually are."

"Think about it, sweetheart," Uncle Edward warned. "He told me just the other day 'this God stuff' wasn't for him. You know what the Bible says . . ."

But Mary Margaret wouldn't listen. "He'll change," she insisted, "I'm sure of it. As soon as we're married, I'll talk him into going to church and he'll come around. You'll see." She kissed Uncle Edward on the cheek and sailed off.

"Aren't you going to forbid it, Edward?" Aunt Rose had asked after she left.

Uncle Edward had sighed and shook his head. "What good would that do, Rose? You know how stubborn she is. She's almost eighteen, and he's twenty-one. They'll just elope and we'll lose her trust. She'll have to learn from her own mistakes."

As we crawled into bed that night, I realized with a heavy heart that Mary Margaret was beginning to learn.

* * *

When my letter finally came, it still wasn't from Jake. At least not directly.

The postman rang the bell exactly two weeks and a day after the disaster. He tipped his hat to Aunt Rose, then saw me standing behind her and nodded in my direction. "Special delivery for you, Mrs. Freeman."

He handed me a thin white envelope. "I'm sure it's good news, ma'am," he said with a smile. "The bad ones don't smell like cologne."

I sniffed the envelope. He was right. There was a distinct smell of after-shave on the paper. But it was nothing I'd ever smelled before.

My heart sank. *What if this isn't from Jake either?*

"Aren't you going to open it?" Aunt Rose prodded me gently.

I ripped open the flap and let the envelope drop to the floor. The stationery was monogrammed with the name "The Royal Hawaiian—Honolulu." I searched the bottom of the page eagerly, but instead of the familiar "Love, Jake," the note was signed "Lt. Com. Lester Drain for Petty Officer 3rd Class Jake Freeman."

"Dear Mrs. Freeman," it read. "Your husband would like you to know he is safe and recuperating well from numerous burns and a wound to his right shoulder. These are trying times and none of us knows when we will be home. Lord willing, your Jake will soon be able to contact you himself."

At least he's alive. I should have felt elated, but instead I felt numb. *What did you expect, girl, "I'm fine and will be home tomorrow"? Yes,* I thought to myself, *that's exactly what I wanted.*

Aunt Rose's eyes welled up when I read the letter to her, but she brushed away the tears and hugged me tight. "Oh, Cissy, I'm so relieved. He'll be home soon, I just know it."

Uncle Edward laughed and swung me around the room. "I told you, Celia. Didn't I tell you? I knew he'd be all right. Thank God!"

Chapter
Eighteen

Dotty sat up straight and held her head high even though, I knew, she was dying inside.

"The doctors warned him not to expect a miracle. They said the chances of him ever walking again were 99 to 1."

I couldn't believe it. We had all hoped—no, expected—that Sam's injuries were temporary. At least I had. How could I ever live with the reality of our Sam in a wheelchair forever? And all because of me!

"Surely there must be some way—?"

Dotty shook her head. "I know he's in a lot of pain, but he never complains. His reading has improved so much he rarely gets things backwards anymore. He says his brain has to make up for his legs."

She brushed a crumb off the sofa and poured us each another cup of tea. "He works so hard and studies half the night, but he won't let me do a thing beyond bringing him a meal now and then. I have to threaten to lock up his books to get him to eat at all." She let out a long sigh. "Listen to me going on and on. At least Sam's healthy otherwise. What about Jake?"

Jake.

"He's already on an airplane headed for the mainland, but we can't pick him up until tomorrow."

My mind had been a whirl for days, one minute excited, the next afraid. He had written only once since those horrible weeks in December: a note scrawled across the face of a post-card that said he missed me and would be home soon. It wasn't until the middle of January that he telephoned to say it would be another month before he was released. "They won't let me out of this blasted place until I get stronger," he said. "And how am I supposed to get stronger if they keep me cooped up in here?"

But he was stronger now. At least strong enough to make the trip from Oahu to Los Angeles.

"You look flushed, Celia. Is it too warm in here? I can open a window."

"No, Dotty, I'm sorry. My mind was just drifting."

She set her cup on the end table. "Come on," she said and pulled me to my feet. "Sam is home by now, and I know he wants to see you. We'll take him the rest of this lemon cake. One thing he can't resist is sugar, and it's so hard to come by. How does your aunt do it?"

Halfway down the hall she put her hand on my arm. "Don't say too much, Celia," she whispered. "Sam's determined; he doesn't want sympathy."

I nodded. Dotty had grown up in the months since gradua-tion. She was still sweet and fun to be around, but now she was also calmer, more capable and obviously very much in love with Sam.

I felt my chest tighten when Sam opened the door. His legs hung motionless, his feet propped against the dull chrome foot-rest on his wheelchair. He'd been studying a heavy tome, a law book of some sort, but he lifted it to the counter with ease. His smile was genuine when he kissed me hello.

"Celia, you look wonderful! It's good to see you. Where's that husband of yours? I thought he'd be here by now." He flashed his gaze to Dotty, who was moving carefully around the cluttered apartment picking up pieces of clothing and newspapers. "Quit fussing, Dot. Come fix us some coffee."

He maneuvered his chair skillfully into the tiny sitting area and cleared the sofa of paper and debris with one sweep of his arm. "Sorry the place is such a mess," he grinned. "Dot keeps after me to clean it up, but . . ." He shrugged and left the sentence go unfinished.

Dotty smiled and laid a hand on his shoulder as she handed him a mug of steaming coffee. Sam looked up at her in gratitude and covered her hand with his free one. "She tries to take care of me, but I'm afraid I'm not a very good patient."

"A stubborn one for sure," Dotty agreed. "I could have this place clean as a whistle in no time, but he won't hear of it." She snatched an empty plate and two cups off the table and danced just out of reach as he tried to swat her backside.

I had to laugh at their antics. It was good to see them so happy. They were both obviously comfortable with their relationship. Dotty was good for Sam. I just hoped he wasn't too stubborn to admit it.

They were both looking at me now, Dotty with genuine concern and Sam with a look I couldn't interpret. "Are you okay, doll? I mean, this thing with Jake. Will any of his injuries be permanent?"

My eyes began to sting, but I forced a smile. I wanted to say, "No. I'm sure he'll be just fine." But I didn't know that.

"I really don't know. He just said he was well enough to come home."

For now, that would have to be enough.

* * *

The Jake who moved so carefully down the hospital steps was not the same Jake who had left over a year before. It wasn't his unsteady movements or the weight loss or the arm that was still strapped to his chest in a heavy cast. It was the way he held his head, the way his eyes darted away from mine. It was the absence of the crooked grin and stoic sense of humor that I'd grown to love so much.

When I first saw him, he pulled me close and buried his face in my hair, but the only tears that fell were mine.

"Let's get out of here." He almost dragged me off my feet as he tried to hurry down the hall.

He pushed my hands away when I tried to steady him. "I'll manage!" His voice held a warning that I somehow knew I'd hear again, and an icy fear clutched my heart.

* * *

"Give him time, sweetheart." Aunt Rose gave the skillet one last swipe with her towel as I wrung out the dishrag in the sink.

Jake was in the living room having coffee with Uncle Edward. The conversation at dinner had been mostly one-sided, with Aunt Rose making sure everybody's plate was full and the rest of us trying to make things comfortable for Jake by avoiding all the questions we really wanted to ask. After one long, awkward silence, Mary Margaret asked to be excused and gathered up her things. They all left shortly after to take her the Hendersons'. She was to spend a week there, tending Elroy and watching the house while the adults went up north for a funeral.

I had thought Jake would open up once we were alone. Instead he flopped down in the wingback chair, rested his head against the velvet fabric and closed his eyes.

"You're tired." I tried to sound cheerful. "Come upstairs and lay down awhile. The bed's all ready."

He grimaced and opened his eyes. "We'll start looking for a place tomorrow. I don't want to put your folks out any longer than necessary."

"But, darling, there's no hurry. Uncle Edward says we're welcome as long as we need to stay."

He sat up quickly, and his eyes darkened with pain. He blinked it away. "You're my wife now, Celia. God knows I may not be much of a husband, but I can provide us with a home of our own."

"Give him time," Aunt Rose told me again later. "There's more than just his body that needs to heal."

That night as I lay in my own twin bed trying to pray and listening to Jake toss and turn, I thought about how happy I'd been when I heard he was alive. I had thanked God on my knees for giving me back my husband, and I had promised I would never doubt him again. Little did I know how impossible it would be for me to keep that promise.

* * *

We found a two-room walkup on the top floor of an apartment building in San Pedro. The rooms were airy and spacious in spite of the grimy exterior. I couldn't help but feel a glimmer of excitement as my eyes combed the empty space. "The sofa will fit against that wall, and Grandpa Freeman's table can go there."

Grandpa Freeman had moved in with Jake's family several months before, when he'd broken his ankle in a fall. "Dangdest thing I ever did!" he declared from his hospital bed. "Fell over my own two feet!

"I'm getting old, boy," he told Jake's pa. "Best take me to the boneyard and shoot me."

Instead, they took him home with them in spite of his protests that he'd never get well "with all the hullabaloo and squallin' that goes on over there."

Grandpa Freeman didn't have many worldly goods, but after he moved Jake and I did wind up with a table, two chairs and a reading lamp. I'd been collecting household things for two years, so we'd do fine with the sofa and bed we'd picked out the day before.

Jake watched from the doorway as I pranced around the rooms trying to decide where things should go. "You'll have the carpet worn out before we move in," was all he said, but I could tell he was pleased.

I ran back to him and put my arms around his waist. "It's perfect, darling. And so close to Dotty and Sam."

He smiled and kissed my hair.

"And close to the hospital too." I felt his body stiffen. Now I'd ruined the mood. I felt a stab of resentment, then pushed it away. *He'll get over it,* I thought and hugged him tighter. *If I love him enough, he'll realize he's better off here, safe, with me.*

Chapter
Nineteen

Dotty had landed a plum job as a typist for the law firm of
Wildish and Hyatt. It was close to the university and, like she
said, kept her up on the terminology so she could talk to Sam.

"It's self-preservation, actually. Otherwise, we'd never be able
to hold a conversation; he'd be speaking Greek to me and I'd
bore him to death."

It felt so good to be close enough to visit with her in person
instead of writing letters all the time. I missed Aunt Rose and
Uncle Edward dreadfully, and having Dotty near helped ease
my homesickness.

A few weeks after Jake and I were settled, she came by the
apartment with news that there was an opening for another
typist. "The kid at the desk next to mine couldn't cut the mustard. She made so many errors, Mr. Wildish lost his temper and
had her in tears for two days. They finally let her go.

"Don't worry," she added, waving away my look of dismay,
"you can handle it. This kid was so green I don't see how she
got the job in the first place." She took a sip of tea. "Come to
think of it, she did have pretty legs."

She grinned and set her cup on the coffee table. "You'll like
Mr. Wildish. He's an older man, a bachelor. But I'm working

on that."

"Dotty!"

She laughed, "Not for me, silly."

"What about the other one?"

"Mr. Hyatt?" She shrugged. "We don't see much of him. He's married with three kids and into politics or something. Rumor has it he's quite a ladies' man, but then I wouldn't know."

She looked so pious, I had to laugh. "One of these days, Dotty Johnson, your 'rumors' are going to get you into trouble."

She let that pass and carried her cup into the kitchen. "Anyway, you're a terrific secretary. The job is really beneath you, but the pay is good."

I followed her. "Ah, Dotty, what would I do without you?"

She looked around the apartment at the empty fruit bowl and half-filled pantry. "Starve." She handed me the bag of apples she'd bought on the way over. "Here, make Jake a dessert. They're sweet enough by themselves if you're out of sugar coupons."

I flushed and she quickly changed the subject. "Anyway, this place is too clean! You need a job."

* * *

Jake wouldn't talk about what happened at Pearl Harbor. At night he thrashed around, held fast in the grip of nightmares he refused to share. By morning the sheets were soaked with sweat. I had to change them every day before I left for work.

"It tries my patience that he won't talk to me about it," I explained to Dotty. "But then I think, 'What if he weren't here at all?' There would be no sheets to change, but no husband either."

She glanced at the family picture I kept on my desk, and we both knew she was looking at Mary Margaret.

At first I tried to ignore it when Jake came home once in a while with liquor on his breath and sullen. He took to smoking cigarettes too, although he was careful not to light up when the family was around. If they smelled it on his clothes, they didn't say a word.

* * *

We took the bus to Uncle Edward's house for Easter. Dotty's folks had come for her and Sam. They were having a houseful of relatives and had included Sam's entire family. Dotty was a wreck before they left.

"I just know someone will ask about a wedding and embarrass us," she fretted as I helped her pack her bag. "You know how stubborn Sam is, he won't even talk about marriage." She pushed a lock of hair behind her ear and bent to buckle the strap on her suitcase. "And yet he says he loves me."

"Ugh. This is heavy." She let go of the handle and collapsed back on her bed.

I smiled. I had begun to believe there was more to Sam's reluctance than met the eye. "Sam's not stubborn, just determined." I shoved the heavy bag toward the door and lay down beside Dotty.

I wanted nothing more than to close my eyes and get some sleep, but Jake would be through with his checkup soon, and I only had a few more minutes to visit. "He has to prove himself. He wants to have a degree in hand and a steady job before he asks you to marry him."

Dotty sighed and rolled over on her stomach. "I know. But do you realize how far away that is? Four years of college, then on to law school." She pounded the pillow with her fist. "He makes me so mad! Can't he see it would be so much easier if we were married now? I could help him get through school, keep the place clean . . . I'm sorry. You've heard this all before, haven't you?" She hopped up off the bed.

I wanted to tell her marriage wasn't the eternal state of bliss she thought it would be. "Don't worry," I said instead, "Sam will come around. Just give him time." Aunt Rose's words echoed in my ears.

* * *

Pastor Stewart's Easter message rang with reverence and authority. We hadn't been to church since Jake's return, and my heart stored up the words like water in an empty well. I tried not to look at Jake. I didn't want him to think I was watching him, but the few times I did glance his way his eyes were fixed on the pastor's face and he seemed to be listening attentively.

Aunt Rose had a solo part in the cantata. When the choir sang the last stanza of my favorite hymn, I heard Jake singing low under his breath, "He lives, he lives, Christ Jesus lives today . . ." He held my hand all the way home.

* * *

Even with all the rationing, Aunt Rose's dinner was a feast. Uncle Edward had traded a case of cookies to the butcher for a nice smoked ham. There were sweet potatoes from the garden, and Mary Margaret had baked biscuits.

"You're getting to be quite a cook," Uncle Edward beamed as he buttered his third one. The butter was just oleo mixed with a drop or two of yellow dye, but we were careful of it just the same and I'd never seen Uncle Edward eat so much. He talked and laughed a lot too.

Finally Aunt Rose flashed him the look she used to give Billy when he was misbehaving at the table. "Slow down, Edward, you'll make yourself ill."

When I thought about it later, I realized he was just trying to put us all at ease. Billy's place was conspicuously empty, and Mary Margaret hadn't heard from Wesley in two months.

The folks had gotten a letter from Billy, though, and Uncle Edward read it to us when gathered in the living room after dinner.

It's cold here and the mud's so deep it runs over my boot tops. We have plenty of provisions, but boy what I wouldn't give for a bowl of Mom's home-cooked stew. We're living in tents for now, but our assignment is to build our own barracks. It won't take us very long. We're all in a hurry to get up off the ground. I don't guess we're in much danger here, but don't worry, Mom, we're ready for them if they come.

Uncle Edward's voice cracked when he read the part about danger, and Aunt Rose had to leave the room. Jake's eyes narrowed to tiny slits. He sat hunched over on the sofa rubbing his cast so hard I thought he'd put a hole in it.

* * *

By May I had started going to church with Dotty and Sam. Jake refused to go. "I'm tired," he'd say and roll over on his side. "You go if it makes you feel better."

Church did more than make me feel better. There wasn't a Sunday that went by but what the sermon seemed to speak to me. The young pastor had just graduated from seminary, but he made God's words hop right off the pages of the Bible and into my soul.

One Sunday in July I came home to find the apartment empty. Jake usually left a note if he went out while I was away, but today the note pad on the kitchen counter was blank. I spent the day stewing over the sermon I'd just heard on temperance and remembering how Papa had changed when he took to drink and how it seemed to me Mama just stood by and let it happen.

"I can't let that happen to Jake and me," I said aloud. "I won't. Please, God, show me what to do."

By the time I heard his key in the lock around eight o'clock that evening, I had worked up the courage to confront Jake with the truth. I had to make him see what he was doing to our marriage.

I had washed all traces of tears from my face and had a pot

of chicken and dumplings boiling on the stove. It was Jake's favorite meal—of the ones we could afford, anyway. I remembered the old saying, "A spoonful of honey makes the medicine go down," and thought chicken and dumplings would serve for Jake.

The front door squeaked and I busied myself at the stove.

"Celia?"

Jake's tone compelled me to look at him. He stood in the middle of the living room, chin up, head cocked to one side, like the boy I'd known when I was thirteen. His mouth twitched with the beginning of a smile, and his eyes brightened as he held out his hand.

Not the left one. The right.

"Jake, your arm!" I dropped the ladle into the pot and ran to him. Instead of moving away, he pulled me to him and kissed me hard.

The arm was white and shriveled, but he could flex his fingers and move his wrist a little. He drew it back when I tried to touch it, so I let it be and hugged him again.

"What happened? Where have you been?" All of my resolve to confront him vanished as I pulled him toward the sofa. "The cast is gone. And no sling! Jake, are you sure—?"

"Slow down, woman, there's still a sling." His eyes darkened, but I was determined not to let the conversation end.

"Jake Freeman, you tell me what is going on! You weren't supposed to get the cast off for another month."

"Okay, okay," his mouth curved in a familiar teasing grin. "But I'm starved, and if my nose is right, my supper's burning on the stove."

"My dumplings!" I ran to the kitchen and snatched the pan off the burner. Some of the chicken had scorched on the bottom, but once we sat down at the table the meal tasted like nectar to me, and Jake lapped it up like a cat drinking cream.

Chapter
Twenty

The light in the living room vanished with the sun, but neither of us moved to turn on a lamp or pull the shades. A cool breeze stirred the curtains at the open windows, bringing with it the smell of the sea.

Jake inhaled deeply. He reached for the pack of cigarettes on the table, then drew his hand away. "Ah, the air smells good." He stretched his legs and propped his feet up on the table. He hadn't told me much about his day except that he'd gone by the hospital to have his arm checked and convinced them to let him go without the cast awhile.

I wiped a drop of sweat from his temple and let my head fall to his shoulder, content to have him near me in the darkness.

"Commander Drain was at the hospital today. You know, the chaplain I told you about."

I wanted to say, "No, you haven't told me much of anything," but I thought it best to keep quiet.

"He walked by just as the doc was unwrapping my arm. Recognized me right away." Jake shifted his weight and pulled me down across his lap. A huge orange moon framed itself in the window and lit up the room. I lay without moving and watched his face change with each emotion as he talked.

"Can you believe that guy? He wrote letters home for over sixty men, but he remembered me."

I realized he must be talking about the man who wrote us from Oahu. "You mean Lester Drain, the lieutenant commander?"

He nodded. "Commander, now. He was promoted in January. If anyone ever deserved it, he did."

He winced and pulled his arm up higher on his chest. *He needs his sling,* I thought, but I couldn't move. His fingers traced a pattern on my cheek, and he lowered his head to look at me. "He asked about you. Wanted to know if you were handling it okay—with my injuries and all. I told him, 'Yes, she's doing fine,' but then I realized I really didn't know. I've never even asked you, have I, babe?"

I could see tears forming in his eyes.

"So, how you doing, Cissy? Are you going to make it through this?"

"Oh, Jake," I grabbed his good hand and brought it to my lips. "We'll both make it. We'll get through it together."

* * *

"The nerves and tendons are damaged from the shoulder to the elbow. There's not much more we can do."

I felt like a sleepwalker in a maze, sitting in the surgeon's office, listening to him pronounce the verdict on Jake's injuries.

Jake sat at attention in the padded chair next to mine. Now and then a muscle in his face twitched—the only sign he even heard what the doctor was saying.

"Physical therapy will help, of course. You'll be able to do a lot more than you think." The doctor rose and moved around his brown steel desk. The paint was chipping on the legs, and the top was covered with a heavy, ink-scarred blotter.

Can't the military even afford to give their doctors better furniture? I shook the foolish thought away. *Of course not, we're at war.*

The captain laid a heavy hand on each of our shoulders. "You two take it easy. Take some time to decide what you'd like to do."

Jake stood, and the captain ushered us toward the door. "I'll see about your discharge."

"No." Jake stopped and spun around, then caught himself. "No, sir. I don't want a discharge. I'd prefer to finish my hitch."

The captain raised his eyebrows. "I see. Well, I don't think it's possible, but I'll look into it." He brought his hand up in salute. "Dismissed, sailor."

Jake turned stiffly on his heel. I almost had to run beside him as he marched down the hallway, through the double doors and out into the street.

*　*　*

Jake spent his days in physical therapy or at the gym on High Street. His burns were almost healed; the skin grafts had taken well, and, except for some scarring on his back and legs, none of his physical wounds was obvious.

I came home from work two weeks after his last doctor's visit to find him standing at the kitchen sink, a sheaf of papers in one hand and a book of matches in the other.

"There's no room in the Navy for a one-armed mechanic." He wouldn't look at me, but I could hear the anger in his voice.

"Jake, stop! You'll burn the house down." I grabbed the smoldering papers and blotted them quickly with a damp dishtowel. He didn't try to stop me as I collected the shreds of an official-looking envelope from the kitchen floor. The papers had DE-PARTMENT OF THE NAVY stamped all over them. I knew without being told what they were.

He slammed his fist into the wall, and a chunk of plaster fell at his feet. "They can't do this. Not now. And I won't let them." His voice dropped, and he looked at me with pain-drenched eyes. "There's a war out there, Celia, and I'm going to fight it.

One way or another, they'll take me back."

I watched him move stiffly toward the bedroom and shuddered. Somehow I knew he'd find a way.

* * *

"He's so stubborn. Why can't he be content with a civilian job?" I complained to Dotty the next day. "Uncle Edward would hire him at the plant, or the Navy would pay for him to finish school."

Dotty smiled and pushed the sugar bowl in my direction. I waved it away. Coffee was already a luxury; I'd feel guilty using up her ration of sugar as well. She shrugged and stirred a heaping teaspoon into her own cup.

"Remember what you said about Sam? 'He's not stubborn, just determined.' I think the same is true for Jake. He's got a lot of battles to fight, and the war is the least of them.

"Jake's a proud man, you've said that yourself. How do you think he feels knowing he can't fight for his country or support his wife the way he wants to?" She sighed. "You and I have a lot in common, kiddo. We both love men who know what they want and are willing to kick life in the teeth to get it."

I knew she was right, but there was a difference too. Sam was willing to trust God to help him over the hurdles; Jake was not. I could only pray that would change.

* * *

Mary Margaret finally got a letter from Wesley. It was dated March 1, 1942, but it wasn't postmarked till July 15.

Sorry, cupcake, there's no way I'll be home for Easter or Fourth of July or Christmas either. In case you hadn't noticed, there's a war going on. I got to keep the stingers polished on this Wasp of mine. We're going to send them yellow devils packing for kingdom come or die trying.

Gotta go. We're out of here tomorrow morning and I've got a few hours of shore duty at the nearest bar. Ha Ha. Keep the home fires burning, kiddo, and try not to miss me too much.

Your ever-loving, Wesley

Mary Margaret took the letter back and stuck it in her purse. "Of course I didn't show it to Mama. She'd have a fit over the stuff about the bar."

She shook a cigarette out of the pack by her elbow and lit it. "Oh, don't look at me like that. I only have one now and then. It calms my nerves." She took a deep breath and shook her head. "When will this stupid war be over? I swear I can't take it one more minute. Wesley's seeing other women, I just know it, and I can't be there to stop him."

She was in one of her surly moods, and I knew there was nothing I could say to change her mind. I waved the smoke out of my eyes. "If you think Aunt Rose would be upset over Wesley going to a bar, how do you think she'd feel about this?" I tossed the cigarettes to the other end of the table. Mary Margaret retrieved the pack and stuck it in her purse with a shrug.

"Jake smokes. And don't think they don't know that!"

I sighed, "Jake *smoked,* Mary Margaret. Past tense. He gave it up a month ago. He said the smoke made it hard for him to breathe when he runs."

"Back to work, you two." Dotty flapped a dishtowel in our direction and pointed toward the kitchen. "The men will be here any minute, and there are still six trays of sandwiches to set out."

Mary Margaret groaned. "How'd I get trapped into this? I work hard enough at the factory. I do my part for the war effort by punching holes in steel." But she got up and followed me into the kitchen.

The three of us had been working at the USO on Front Street for two months now. I liked it. And it gave me something productive to do, since Jake was gone most evenings. Sometimes he played cards with Sam, and sometimes he didn't tell me where he'd been. "You need to get out some too, Celia," he told me. "Why don't you see if Dotty needs any help at the USO?"

"The more the merrier," Dotty had chimed in, glad to except my offer. "We'll get Mary Margaret too."

I was pretty skeptical about the odds of *that,* but, to my surprise, Mary Margaret had jumped on the idea. "Of course I will," she said, preening. "Those poor boys need someone to dance with."

Mary Margaret was a beautiful woman and a good dancer too. I knew it was hard for her to sit home at night. Darning socks and rolling bandages wasn't her cup of tea. But I worried about her dancing with all those men when Wesley was so far away.

"What if she falls for one of them?" I asked Jake. "Wesley would find out and divorce her in a minute."

"Would that be so bad?"

He ducked the pillow I threw and tackled me, dropping us both on top of the cherry pattern quilt Aunt Rose had given us for our first anniversary.

He held my arms and kissed me soundly, then kissed me again. Just before he kissed me the third time, I realized his grip on my left arm was almost as strong as the one on my right.

Chapter
Twenty-one

Grandpa Freeman passed away in August. Jake's father picked us up the morning of the funeral. He looked like a different person in a stiff white shirt, brown tweed pants and a borrowed brown jacket that was at least one size too small.

"Thing itches like the dickens," he complained, "and it's already hotter than h—hades outside."

We pulled into the driveway, and my heart lurched with the engine of the pickup when Mr. Freeman turned the key off. The hedge between the houses had grown two feet and looked like no one had pruned it in years. I could still see the house, though. Our house. It looked smaller than I remembered. Someone had painted it an ugly yellow and left the porch and railings gray.

The hill doesn't look as steep either, and the sidewalk's too bumpy to skate on. The yard was littered with trash and toys and a small red wagon that could have been Chuckie's.

I blinked and looked away.

The shed where Papa had kept the Nash stood empty. Some of the boards had fallen down, and the back part of the roof caved in. I could still see Jake hunched down in the corner lifting a bottle of Papa's whiskey to his lips, his eyes glinting with mischief as he offered me some.

I felt Jake's arm come around my waist and realized we were out of the truck. Mr. Freeman had gone inside, and my reverie was soon broken by the slam of a screen door and a tangle of arms and legs as bodies big and small clamored for kisses and hugs.

None of the Freemans was ever shy. The two littlest climbed Jake's legs like monkeys in a circus. The older girls kissed my cheek and fought to hold my hands as we made our way toward the house.

The screen door banged again as Mrs. Freeman tottered toward us. Her two-inch heels kept getting stuck in the cracks between the boards of the wooden porch. She finally kicked them off, and I found myself being smothered by her ample bosom.

"Let me look at you, child," she crowed and pushed me to arm's length. "I haven't seen hide nor hair of you since the day Jake come home."

I felt my face flush and looked guiltily at Jake. Could it be true that I hadn't visited in almost seven months? But she was right. Oh, they'd seen Jake. He'd gone over several times while I was at work, and his father had helped us move. But I'd been so busy and she had such a houseful . . .

"Oh, Mother Freeman, I'm so sorry. I never dreamed it had been so long."

"Land, child, I understand. You got your hands full taking care of this boy of mine." She ruffled Jake's hair and pried one of the little ones off his leg.

"Into the house, Davy, and wash those hands!" She swatted at his backside and missed by a mile as the child squealed in delight and raced through the screen door. "And you two go brush your hair. It's almost time to go. You want to make your granddaddy proud?" Two blond heads nodded in unison. The girls let go of my hands and raced for the house.

Mrs. Freeman sighed and held my arm to steady herself while she stepped back into her shoes. "These things are just torture machines. Haven't worn them in nigh on twenty years, and I hope to never wear them again." Once inside, she waved us toward the cluttered sofa. "And Celia"—I pushed aside a stack of diapers and looked up at her—"you might as well call me Ma. Lord knows everybody does."

Tim was gone. He'd turned nineteen in October 1942 and, fearing the draft, had enlisted about the same time as Billy, only in the Marines.

The next in line was Jake's oldest sister, Anne Marie. She was a beauty with shiny dark hair and eyes that I was sure would melt a thousand hearts. She had graduated with honors from Freemont High and was studying to be a nurse. "One more year," she replied shyly when I asked her how long she'd be in nursing school. "I'd like to help out in the war, but Ma won't let me go. Says she needs my help around here."

I looked around the cluttered room and understood why. There were six other siblings, ages three to fifteen. With Jake gone and now Tim . . .

"Land sakes, I can't do a thing with that child." Mrs. Freeman tottered into the room fussing with the buttons on a soiled coat. Her eyes lit up when she saw Anne Marie.

"Annie M., go help your brother find his other shoe. We got to get to the cemetery." She didn't specify which brother, but that didn't seem to bother Anne. She flashed a weak smile in my direction and headed for the stairs.

I looked at Mrs. Freeman and tried to imagine Anne in ten or even twenty years, but I couldn't make a comparison. Jake's mama had a hard life, with so many kids and never enough money to make ends meet. When I had first met her, I almost pitied her. But as I got to know her better I realized there was always a spark of laughter in her eyes—and enough love in that ample bosom to mother a hundred little ones.

After the graveside service, Jake hustled us away as soon as possible. "It's all right, Pa," he said, waving away his father's halfhearted offer to drive us. "We'll take the bus. It's not that far."

As the bus lurched away from the corner stop, I caught my breath and said, "Jake Freeman, that was rude!" Straightening my hat, I added, "We could have at least stayed for pie."

Jake just shrugged. "It's a madhouse over there. Gives me a headache."

I realized my own head was pounding and linked my arm with Jake's. "It *is* a little overwhelming. And your ma kept asking if I was in the family way! When I told her no, she patted my hand and said, 'Don't fret about it. You'll soon have a whole litter. One thing about the Freeman men; they're virile.' Can you imagine?" I laughed and poked Jake in the ribs, but he didn't smile.

"I've wondered about that too."

"What?"

"You know, why you're not . . . Oh, never mind." He closed his eyes and laid his head back against the seat.

I let it be. To tell the truth, I'd thought about it a lot lately myself. We'd never really talked about having children. I just assumed the Lord would send them in his own good time. *But what if something's wrong with me?* I pushed the thought away. *Of course, it's just as well. With Jake's uncertain future, we don't need another mouth to feed.*

We didn't talk about it again. Not for a long time.

* * *

Back in April, the carrier *Hornet* had launched Jimmy Doolittle's B-25 bombers for an attack on Tokyo. Jake followed that and other news of the war with a mixture of enthusiasm and personal defeat. He never spoke of it, but we both knew his dream of being a pilot was over.

The battle for the Coral Sea and the Japanese defeat at Midway Island had spurred his efforts to recover. Now, in late August, we'd heard rumors of another invasion, and Jake's restlessness returned full force.

"Are you sure that's where they are?" Uncle Edward and Jake sat hunched over the world map spread out in the middle of Aunt Rose's living room.

Jake nodded. "This is where Billy has to be. Anyway, it makes sense. After Midway the next step would be the Solomons. MacArthur would expect to reclaim all the islands. I would bet Nimitz has most of the Navy there too. Although Wesley's ship could be anywhere in the Pacific."

Billy's letters were so heavily marked-up, I didn't see how they could come to any conclusions about his whereabouts. But the news reports were full of talk about a horrible island—"a steamy hellhole fraught with alligators, snakes and enough bugs to sink the state of California," one correspondent revealed.

"That was a slip-up he'll hear about for sure!" Jake declared after we heard the report. "But it pinpoints the action for us."

Aunt Rose came in and set a shallow dish with a single camellia blossom in the center of the table. She stood back to admire it, adjusted the angle of the doily underneath and turned toward the living room. "Edward, please. The boys will be here any minute, and this room's a mess. They're here to be part of a family and have a home-cooked meal. I'm sure they see enough maps at the base."

When we'd arrived an hour earlier, Aunt Rose had informed us there'd be company for dinner.

"Some of the boys from the air base, dear. I hope you don't mind." She turned to Jake. "One of them is a friend of Billy's. He joined the air corps after basic training. I thought you might have some things in common."

Jake looked like he'd bolt for the door any minute, but Aunt Rose had already hustled back to the kitchen and didn't notice.

Jake, please. He seemed to understand the look in my eyes and sat back down on the sofa. Then Uncle Edward had brought out Billy's last letter and the map.

Now they rolled the map back up and put it in a cardboard tube. Uncle Edward carried it upstairs.

Mary Margaret came down just in time to answer the door. I could tell she was disappointed when she saw how young the boys were. There were two of them, and both were dressed in tan pants and short-sleeved shirts. They stood practically at attention in the doorway, hats in hand, eyes forward, blushing under Mary Margaret's searching gaze.

"Well, let them in, dear. Come in, come in, we're glad to have you." Aunt Rose shooed Mary Margaret away and ushered the two young men into the living room.

After introductions, everyone seemed more relaxed. By the time we sat down to the table, even Jake was smiling and talking up a storm.

"They're just youngsters," he said on the way home. "We're sending babies to do a man's job."

"Like Billy?" I still couldn't believe the government had let him enlist, let alone sent him into battle. I could hardly stand to hear Jake and Uncle Edward talking about us taking over the Pacific islands. I thought Aunt Rose was better off not knowing where Billy was or what he was up to.

Jake didn't answer. He seemed lost in a dream world the rest of the way home. A world where, as I'd already learned, I couldn't follow.

Chapter
Twenty-two

I never knew till later that Jake was seeing Commander Drain almost every day. We'd gone together to see him once or twice "just to talk," Jake had said. "He asked to meet you. I think you'll like him, Celia."

The chaplain was about thirty-five, with short dark hair just showing gray around the temples. He had a ready smile and soft brown eyes. When he looked at you, you could tell that he was really listening and interested in what you had to say. I knew Jake liked him, and I could see why. He was open and honest, a caring man who lived his faith. "He reminds me of Uncle Edward," I told Jake one day.

Jake looked thoughtful, then nodded. "Yes, I guess he does."

* * *

September was a scorcher. Jake and I went back to Bear Lake one Saturday, but the rocks were crowded with young mothers in bathing suits, basting their bodies with baby oil and yelling at small children. The boat rental shack was boarded up, a "No Trespassing" sign nailed to the front. "The old man probably croaked," Jake said with a shrug and stuck his hands deep into the pockets of his dungarees. *And his sons went off to war.* I buried the thought and took Jake's arm.

Farther down the beach, some soldiers from the air base were lighting firecrackers and tossing them into the water. They turned and stared when they caught sight of us, and I held tighter to Jake's arm. I thought maybe we would know some of them from Aunt Rose's dinner parties. She and Uncle Edward served meals to "the boys" at least once a week and gave some of them a place to sleep when it was needed.

"It's like having Billy home," Aunt Rose told me once. "Besides, it's the least we can do for the war effort."

None of the faces was familiar, but Jake stood solid as a statue and returned them stare for stare until one of them lit another cracker and threw it far out into the water. The rest turned back to their game. I tugged on Jake's arm. He came away with me, but hours later I could still see the defiance in his eyes.

"It's like the thorn that festered in the lion's paw," I told Dotty the next morning, "but my lion won't let anybody pluck it out."

She rolled another sheet of paper into her typewriter. "Don't worry, honey, when it gets sore enough he'll pop it out himself."

I knew she was right, but I wasn't sure I wanted to be around when he did.

* * *

Before I knew it Halloween was over and Thanksgiving too. One rainy Sunday in December, I realized that it had been almost a year since Pearl Harbor.

We made popcorn and fruit cups at the USO that night. Sam was buried in his studies for a test on Monday morning, and Jake disappeared right after dinner.

"I'm going over to the base," he announced as he grabbed his jacket off the coat rack by the door. "I may be late, so don't wait up." He brushed his lips across my cheek, and I had to bite my tongue to keep from asking why. He never answered questions about his doings at the base, just brushed them off with a joke or some caustic remark, depending on his mood. "Don't you trust me?" he'd ask and flash a teasing grin. "Of course I do," I'd say. "It's just . . ." But he'd be out the door before I could finish my sentence.

The last time I questioned him, he must have had a bad day because he yelled, "Can't a man have any privacy, for Pete's sake?" and slammed the door so hard Grandma Eva's sampler fell off the wall.

"It can't be too bad," Dotty assured me when I complained. "You said he comes home sober and usually in a better mood than when he left. Whatever it is, it must be good for him."

"Hmph. Whatever it is, it's probably too good for him!" Mary Margaret appeared from behind a crate, broke open a sack of popcorn and poured some in the popper. "If you ask me, Celia, you should follow him. Any man that won't say where he's going and comes home happy has a chicky in the wings somewhere."

I fought the urge to slap her. Of course I'd thought of that, but Jake had never shown signs of wanting other women. He was always home for dinner, and when he said, "I love you," it rang true. I'd heard Grandma Eva tell Mama, "The best way to hold your man is with good food and lots of prayer." I didn't understand it then, but I'd been following her advice for months. Jake had even been attending Sunday services with Dotty, Sam and me. "Not Jake," I finally said aloud.

"Why not Jake?" Mary Margaret spun around, and I could see the pain in her eyes. "What makes him such a perfect saint?"

"Button your lip, girl." Dotty threw a dishrag toward the sink. It missed Mary Margaret but splashed water all over her face and hair. Her mouth dropped open, and before either Dotty or I could move, she burst into tears and ran screeching from the room.

"Oh, Celia, I'm sorry . . ." Dotty's eyes were huge.

I untied my apron. "Don't worry, I'll find her."

But by the time I ran out to the street she was nowhere in sight.

* * *

Jake came home at ten and crawled into bed next to me. His face was drawn, and he looked so tired I didn't have the heart to tell him I was worried about Mary Margaret. I'd taken a taxi all the way to the boarding house, but her landlady said she hadn't seen her since that morning. I'd thought about calling Uncle Edward, but I was pretty sure that would be the last place she'd turn up, and I didn't want to scare them so I let it be.

"I'm beat, babe. It's been a long night." Jake cupped my chin in his hand, kissed me good-night and rolled over on his side. I curled up next to him and caught the faint aroma of cologne. *No—after-shave.* Not Jake's. I'd smelled it before, but for the life of me I couldn't remember where.

Then I prayed for Mary Margaret and Dotty and Sam. I asked God to watch over Billy and all the others who were at war. I even prayed for Wesley. "There has to be a way, Lord, for you to get his attention; you know Mary Margaret needs her husband." I had just said "Amen" when it hit me.

Commander Drain! That scent was on the chaplain's letter when he wrote for Jake. I'd smelled it again the last time we were in his office. *Is that where Jake's been spending his time?* I felt an instant peace and knew I'd found the truth.

* * *

Jake's screams woke me at midnight. I yanked the covers off and shook him like I always did, but he wouldn't wake up. His skin was clammy and he gasped for breath, like a dog I saw once who'd swallowed a bone. The dog had died right there on the sidewalk with a dozen people standing by.

"Jake! Wake up, you hear me?" I shook him hard and thumped him on the chest.

He gasped and pushed my hands away, then grabbed my wrists and threw me off the bed. He wouldn't let me go, but rolled to the floor on top of me. He was too strong, I couldn't break away as he began to sob and pull me across the room. "Don't die, don't die, don't die!" he pleaded in a voice so hoarse I could hardly understand him.

Suddenly he stopped and lay panting on the carpet next to me. He was sweating profusely and making gurgling noises in his throat. My wrists hurt, but I pushed to my hands and knees. "Jake," I was sobbing now, "wake up. Oh please wake up. You're all right, it's just a dream."

"Celia?"

He was awake. "Thank God," I whispered and let myself collapse beside him on the floor.

He lay still, breathing rapidly for several minutes. I let my own breathing slow to normal and tried to gather my wits about me.

"Did I hurt you?"

His voice startled me. "No. I mean, not really. Are you all right?" I struggled to lean over him. He pulled me close and held me.

"Tell me, Jake. Please, can't you tell me about your dreams?"

He sat up. "Not here. You're freezing." He stood, drew me to my feet and led me back to bed. He tucked the covers close around me and went into the bathroom. I heard the water running, and he returned with a glass for each of us. I realized my mouth was dry as a desert and drank it gratefully.

By the time he crawled back into bed, we had both calmed down. We lay close, but not quite touching. When he finally spoke, it was slowly, deliberately, in a tone I had never heard him use before.

"It was a liberty night," he began. "I'd already sent you a telegram, and my bag was packed ready for the trip home. There was a 'Battle of the Bands' scheduled in the receiving station at Pearl. My buddy Roy and I decided to go. We got there in time to hear the competition for 'I Don't Want to Set the World on Fire' and met some of the guys from the *Arizona*. Their band walked away with second place. Their reward was to sleep in the next morning."

Jake's voice broke, and I thought maybe he would stop, but he took a deep breath and went on.

"Some of the officers were going to a party at Lieutenant Dare's. He and his wife celebrated their anniversary every month. Can you imagine?" he chuckled. "Just an excuse to get snockered on champagne, but some of them ended up too drunk to go back to the ship. It saved their lives.

"We weren't invited to the party. None of the swabs were, but the night was still young and most of the guys headed uptown to Hotel Street to get drunk and buy souvenirs. Roy and I wound up at the Swanky Franky, a hot-dog joint. We had an eating contest. I had to stop at six, but Roy managed to swallow eight dogs and about a gallon of beer. He didn't keep it down long, and the manager finally offered me a free Coke if I'd take him out of there.

"I poured coffee down him and walked him around awhile till he finally sobered up. We wound up at a curio shop. I bought you a satin pillow and blew a fiver on Skee-Ball at the shooting gallery."

The room grew quiet, and Jake's breathing slowed. I thought he'd gone back to sleep, but when I reached for a hankie to dry my eyes, he spoke again, his voice so low I had to strain to listen.

"We had watch together the next morning, Roy and I, so we

went back to the *West Virginia* early. The *Arizona* crew was still partying in Honolulu. I never saw any of them again.

"I heard them, though. At midnight bands played the national anthem, and soon after that the liberty ships came pouring in. The guys were singing and laughing and jumping in the water. A few shipmates came stumbling in, bumping into bunks in the dark. The same old normal Saturday night, except I remember wishing they'd just can it and let me sleep. I was dreaming about you, babe, and I wanted to go back and finish the dream."

He sighed and stretched out his arm. I took the cue and laid my head against his chest in the hollow between his neck and shoulder. When he held me like that I felt safe and loved, but tonight I knew it was Jake who needed to feel safe.

I stroked his chest and waited for him to talk about the next morning. Commander Drain had told me privately that Jake would feel better when he could finally talk about that day. In the silence I heard the soft whir of my wind-up clock, then a click as the hands turned to mark the hour. Jake's body went slack, his breathing evened out, and the arm that held me fell away. I rolled over and looked at the clock. Two o'clock.

I was still staring at it when the alarm went off at six.

Chapter
Twenty-three

The last thing I wanted to do was go to work. I knew there was more to the story. Jake hadn't even touched on the day of the attack, and, as horrible as it would be, I knew he had to tell it. *Dear God,* I prayed, *please let this be the breakthrough we've been waiting for.*

Jake hadn't moved in five hours, and I didn't have the heart to wake him; it was the first real rest he'd had in a long time. I left him sleeping and dragged myself down to Wildish and Hyatt, in a panic because I was ten minutes late.

Mr. Wildish stuck his head out of his office and looked pointedly at the watch fob hanging from his pocket. It had belonged to his father and he wore it proudly, taking delight in telling its history to anyone who would listen. Most of the secretaries saw him as old-fashioned. "A grumpy old codger," they said behind his back. But Dotty adored him.

I tried a smile. "Sorry, sir, I missed the bus." I hurried by him to my desk.

Dotty looked relieved when she saw me coming. "Did you find her?" she mouthed.

I realized she meant Mary Margaret and shook my head.

Mr. Wildish cleared his throat and disappeared into his office.

I planned to call the Douglas Aircraft factory on my break and see if she was there. I knew they wouldn't let me talk to her unless it was an emergency, so I fiddled with the papers on my desk and tried to think up an excuse to get her to the phone. I was sure Dotty would have some ideas, but Jake showed up at ten minutes after nine and nipped the whole thing in the bud.

He strolled through the door like he owned the place. Dotty nearly dropped her teeth. She told me later Jake looked so serious she thought maybe the mob was after us again.

As he came toward my desk it struck me again how handsome he was. Clean-shaven, dressed in dungarees and a new white shirt open at the neck, he took my breath away.

"Celia, I have to talk to you."

Marie, the receptionist, had followed him through the door. "I tried to stop him," she wailed as Mr. Wildish stuck his head out of his office for the second time.

I grabbed my bag and took Jake's outstretched hand. I knew everyone was watching, and I didn't care. It was like that night at the graduation party, the night he proposed. I saw only that my husband needed me and nothing else mattered. Nothing at all.

"See here, young man, you can't just—"

Mr. Wildish's objection was cut off as the doors shut behind us. Jake led me down the hall, out of the building and onto the windy street. We caught the first bus headed toward Long Beach, and neither of us said a word until we stood at the water's edge.

* * *

A cool breeze blew drops of rain into our faces. Jake put on his overcoat, fastened the buttons on my jacket and helped me tie a scarf around my head. "Let's walk," he said, finally breaking the silence. He turned and headed away from the harbor.

I ran a few steps to catch up with him, then he slowed his pace to match mine and began to talk.

"Roy and I were standing watch on deck. It was a clear morning, balmy, but the sea was calm as a mill pond. I remember thinking how great it would be to have you there beside me. I even joked with Roy about it, told him I'd take you over him any day.

"The bands and color guards had started to assemble on the decks. It was almost 0755, and we were waiting for the signalman in the tower to raise the 'prep' flag."

He must have seen my puzzled look.

"That's the white-and-blue flag," he explained. "It signals the warships to raise the Stars and Stripes in exactly five minutes. It's done in unison, and the bands all play. It's quite a sight, Celia, one you never forget once you've seen it."

I nodded and he went on. "We were moored pretty far north of the tower, close to Ford Island, tied up outboard of the *Tennessee*. The *Maryland* and *Oklahoma* were tied forward and the *Arizona* was about seventy-five feet astern.

"The next thing I knew the air was alive with buzzing planes. It was like they just exploded out of the sun. We were on deck at the stern. I lifted my glasses and saw what looked like an explosion in a hanger at Wheeler Field, then they came toward us, torpedo bombers flying low. I could see red circles on the bomber wings, but I guess it didn't register.

"I yelled at Roy, 'Are we having a drill?' He hollered back, 'If we are, somebody's botched it!'

"Right then someone sounded general quarters. I told Roy we better get to battle stations. I still thought we were having an exercise. But before we could move, one of the planes flew directly overhead and dropped a torpedo in the water. The explosion knocked me sideways through the hatch.

"That's when I knew it was for real."

Jake took my elbow and steered me underneath a pier. "Are you cold?" I shook my head, but he unbuttoned his pea coat and wrapped it around both of us.

"I could smell smoke," he continued, "that heavy rancid smell of burning oil. The ship had started listing toward port, so I grabbed the railing and clawed my way topside. Just as I hit the deck I heard another loud explosion. I watched the *Arizona* leap out of the water like a giant dolphin and burst into a ball of flames.

"Dead men fell out of the sky. Body parts, deck shoes and scraps of clothing. I yelled for Roy, but he wasn't there. I scrambled for the railing, but we took another hit. There were fires everywhere. Someone yelled at me to man a hose. I don't remember how, but I made it to my station.

"It seemed like we fought the flames for an eternity. They kept on coming at us with machine-gun fire and air-to-sea torpedoes. The strafing was so loud I couldn't hear anything else. The only thing that helped was knowing we were firing back.

"Someone tried to grab my hose away, but I couldn't let it go. Shipmates were still running toward us from the hatches, their clothes and hair on fire. I didn't recognize anyone. They all had blackened faces with white flecks for eyes and bloody red gashes where their mouths should have been. We hosed them down, one after another, until all power on the ship was lost.

"The fires were out of control and someone hollered, 'Abandon ship!' The shipmate next to me grabbed my arm and started pulling me portside. I must have screamed. The pain was terrible, but I honestly don't remember being hit. He let me go, but everyone was running in the same direction and I got caught up in the rush.

"Later, I learned there were motor launches from the *California* rescuing the wounded. The list was slight, but some of the men were jumping from the 'Wee Vee' to the *Tennessee*. The sea blazed from burning oil, but men were diving in anyway to swim ashore. I was still pretty far aft when I saw a man in the water right below me. Honest to Pete, Celia, it looked like Roy. He was floundering in the flames, going under, his face alive with fear.

"I didn't even think. Just grabbed the railing and jumped. I landed next to him, and the heat and fumes nearly knocked me out. I grabbed for him, but my arm wouldn't work. He looked right at me and went under one more time."

Jake was shaking visibly now, his hands gripping my upper arms, the nails digging into my skin. I bit my lip, but I didn't speak. I was afraid. I didn't want him to stop, but I didn't want him to go on either.

"I prayed, Celia," he whispered, "I prayed like I'd never prayed before. I thought God had answered. Ford Island was only a few yards away. All I had to do was turn my head to see the shore. I dived under and grabbed him with my left arm just below his chin. My right arm still refused to move, so I rolled to my back and started kicking like mad.

"I remember yelling at him, 'Don't die, don't die!' Then someone pulled us from the water and dragged us both up the beach. They tried to take him away from me, but the chaplain told me later I wouldn't let him go. They said I was screaming like a madman. They had to pry my arm from around his neck. 'It's too late, son, let him go, you're strangling a dead man,' they told me."

Jake's body went slack, and he stayed quiet for a long time. I couldn't move. I had visions of them finding us in the morning, frozen together, entombed in a Navy pea coat, like Roy Cummings in the pickle barrel. Like Jake's buddy Roy on a dirty, blood-soaked beach.

Chapter
Twenty-four

It **was obvious** to me Jake thought he'd killed that man. The chaplain swore to him it wasn't Roy and that whoever it was had died before Jake got him in to shore.

"But how would he know, Celia?" Jake demanded. "How in hades could he know?"

"Why don't you ask him, darling? He wouldn't lie to you. He must have reason to believe it wasn't Roy."

We were sitting in a restaurant, eating breakfast and watching the fog blot out the morning. The water, sand and sky blended into a single gray sheet, an empty canvas waiting for the painter's brush. Jake's voice was just as empty of emotion. His face was still white and drawn from our ordeal the day before.

We had managed to walk to a small hotel a block or so from the beach. I knew we couldn't afford it, and it seemed a waste with our own apartment only a short bus ride away. But Jake was spent. We were cold and wet, and I was sure we'd both have pneumonia by the time we made it home.

"It can be our Christmas present to each other," I assured him as we staggered through the door.

"Got caught in the storm, I see." The old lady at the desk

looked hesitant as she pushed the register in our direction. She took note of the ring on my finger as I paid her, and she reluctantly handed Jake a key. "Any luggage?" When I shook my head she smirked and pointed toward the stairs. "Turn left at the top; it's the first door on the right. Keep the shades down. And no lights! Blackout starts at dusk. The café starts serving breakfast at seven." I could feel her eyes following us up the stairs.

Jake slept for sixteen hours. I took a hot bath and hung our clothes around the radiator to dry. I found an extra blanket on the shelf above the clothes rack and curled up in a faded easy chair.

The room had been pretty once. The chair and bedspread, patterned in the same floral print, were faded now and dingy. A black shade had been nailed above the window under heavy drapes that once had matched the bedspread and the chair. Next to the bed, a rough wooden table supported a brass lamp with a flimsy pleated shade. The bulb had been removed, and a light switch by the door was covered with layers of thick black tape.

In spite of the desk clerk's warning, I raised the shade a few inches and rubbed a clear spot on the dusty window. It was still early afternoon. The rain had stopped, and clouds scurried across a blotchy sky, in a hurry to outrun the gusts of wind that kicked up sand in little whirling funnels and flung it into the air.

I was too tired to sleep. Instead I turned and watched Jake, his body finally relaxed, dark lashes drooped against pale cheeks, mouth opened slightly in a gentle snore.

He lay on his side, facing me, knees drawn up beneath the covers, his left arm under his head, the right curled against his chest as if still in its sling. I knew the position was deceptive. The skin on his injured arm was smooth and taut over firm muscles. His body was still marked by puckered scars, but his right arm was almost as strong as his left.

Still, he looked so vulnerable lying there. I wanted to hold him, to stroke his hair and whisper, *It's okay. It wasn't Roy; it couldn't have been. Roy was killed by the first explosion. And whoever you pulled ashore was dead before you even touched him.*

My eyes shifted. Someone had left a recent copy of *Life* on the table next to the darkened lamp. I held it close to the window and turned the pages in the half-darkness. A full-page picture near the center leaped out at me. A smoking ship, foundering in a choppy sea, a smaller boat pulled up alongside, rescuers hauling sailors from the water.

I fished in the drawer, found a flashlight and focused its beam on the page. A caption at the side read: "One year ago, December 7, 1941. The battleship *West Virginia,* her decks awash, sinks alongside her mooring shortly after being struck by Japanese torpedoes at Pearl Harbor."

"Her casualties were light," the column read. "2 officers, 103 enlisted men were killed or missing."

On the *Arizona* the count was much higher. Almost everyone aboard had died.

The magazine was dated two days ago, and I realized this must have been what tripped Jake's memory and triggered today's ordeal.

I set the magazine aside and lay down next to Jake, still wrapped in my own blanket. He moaned and shifted to his back. I was there for what seemed like hours, watching him sleep and praying for God to heal his deeper wounds.

Now, the next morning, the waitress poured us each another cup of coffee. Jake took a sip and winced as the hot liquid burned his lip. "We'll never know for sure, babe. Let's just leave it at that."

I didn't want to leave it. *How can he ever be whole again until he knows for sure?*

But that day God wasn't giving any answers.

As soon as we got home, I tried to call Mary Margaret. Her landlady assured me she'd been home the night before and had gone to work this morning as usual. Then I called Wildish and Hyatt and asked the switchboard operator to get a message to Dotty.

"Don't worry, honey, I'll have her call you at break. I'm glad you're all right," she chuckled. "That young man of yours caused quite a stir."

Jake was in the tub when Dotty called.

"Boy, am I glad you're back!" She sounded like she'd run around the block four times before dialing. "Mr. Wildish is in a snit. I tried to cover—told him you had a family emergency. I wasn't lying was I, Celia? Sam told me Jake was all upset the other night, but he wouldn't tell me why. Are you okay, girl?"

"I'll explain later," I told her when she finally ran out of breath. "Tell Mr. Wildish I'll be back tomorrow."

"Okay," she huffed, "but I'm not waiting till tomorrow! You and Jake come over tonight. I'll hide Sam's books and we can play cards or something."

I heard the buzzer sound in the background. "Uh-oh. Gotta go. Mr. Wildish will bust a gizzard if I turn up missing too. See you tonight at seven." The phone went dead.

Jake was staring in the bathroom mirror, kneading the muscles in his right shoulder and flexing the fingers on that hand. I slid my arms around his waist and buried my face against his back. His skin felt damp, and I inhaled the sharp clean smell of Lux soap.

"Is the pain still bad?"

He drew a deep breath. "It's been worse."

He turned and took me in his arms. I ran my hands across his shoulders, down his biceps to his chest. I watched his face as I traced the burn scars from his belly to his back. He winced one time, then smiled. "I'm okay, babe. I told you, the pain is almost gone."

When I told him about Dotty's invitation, Jake surprised me by seeming eager to go out. "We've been lazy long enough," he said, trying to swat me with a towel.

I danced out of reach and dialed Mary Margaret again. This time she answered on the third ring. "Where have you been?" She sounded annoyed. "I've been trying to get you for two days."

I knew that wasn't true; we'd only been gone for one. But I ignored her tone. "Jake and I went to the beach," I said and hurried on before she could interrupt. "I've been calling you too. Dot and I were worried sick the other night." I paused, but there was only silence on the other end. "I'm sorry, Mary Margaret, I really am. Dotty and I never meant to hurt your feelings."

I could hear her sniffle. "I know. I'm sorry too. It's just that . . . I'm so worried about Wesley, I could bust."

I felt torn. I knew we should offer to go over there and keep her company tonight, but Jake could hardly stand to be around her. I couldn't blame him. Mary Margaret had been impossible lately, and besides, I really wanted to go to Dotty's.

Mary Margaret solved my problem. "I'm sorry, but I have to go. Daddy's picking me up in an hour. He and Mother promised to take me out to dinner." She sighed. "I know they'll just nag me about going back to church and want to know why I haven't heard from Wesley. I don't know why they care. They've always hated him."

I almost blurted out, "That's not true!" But I kept quiet. From her point of view, it was. She'd got herself so mixed up she couldn't tell who really loved her.

"That man has used her from the start!" I complained to Jake on the bus ride to Dotty's. "Why can't she see what a creep he is?"

"He's her husband, Celia," he said sternly, but he took my hand. "I'll talk to her tomorrow."

I couldn't believe my ears. I wanted to ask him *How?* and *Why?* But the bus hissed to a stop in front of the university, and Jake was already leading me down the aisle.

Chapter
Twenty-five

Jake kept his promise to talk to Mary Margaret. Neither one would tell me what was said, but she was easier to be around afterward—more civil to her parents and not so snooty to the rest of us.

Mr. Hyatt was in Mr. Wildish's office the next morning. I tried to sneak past them to my desk, but before I got two feet into the room, my boss's head popped through the doorway.

"Ah, Mrs. Freeman. If you don't mind?" He waved the papers in his hand like a theater usher with a flashlight, and I had no choice but to enter "the lair," as the other girls called it.

The room was small and boxlike. The dark brown interior made it shrink even more until I felt like I was crammed into a matchbox with a couple of piranhas.

Mr. Hyatt stood beside the desk, arms folded across his chest, a smile flicking on and off. He was a big man, younger than his partner by twenty years. And good-looking in a phony sort of way. He was clean-shaven and wore his dark hair slicked back behind his ears. Dotty swore he dyed it and had his nails manicured every week.

"Rumor has it he's running for Congress," she had said just yesterday. "I'll bet that's why we haven't seen him around."

Now he nodded and offered me the only chair in the room. "Please sit down, Mrs. Freeman—Celia, isn't it? May I call you Celia?" He didn't wait for my answer but looked at Mr. Wildish, who harumphed and settled himself with some effort into the chair behind the desk.

"Well, my dear, may we assume you have your family life in order and are ready to return to work?"

I nodded, wondering what Dotty had told him. "Yes, sir. And I'm sorry about the other day. I had no idea my husband was coming."

His cheeks turned red. "Yes. Well, let's try and give more notice next time." He motioned toward the door. "You'll find a stack of briefs on your desk. I'll need them this afternoon."

Mr. Hyatt reached past me and opened the door. "Good day, Celia." He was smiling broadly now. "I certainly hope we meet again."

"What an odd man," I told Dotty later. "He reminds me of someone. I can't think who, but he gives me the creeps."

"He's probably sweet on you." She grinned and ducked as I threw a paper clip in her direction.

* * *

"I'll be home for Christ-mas . . . If only in my dre—eams."

Bing Crosby warbled the last notes of his latest hit, and the needle on the old Victrola scratched into the empty grooves. No one in the room moved to change the record. We were all too full, but mostly we were all too sad.

Neither Billy nor Wesley had come home, of course, but Uncle Edward had picked Mama up the evening before. She'd spent the night in my old room. I closed my eyes and imagined families around the country sitting just like this, lonesome for their loved ones and tired of hearing nothing but talk about the war.

Jake finally stood and moved the needle arm off the spinning record. "I think I'll take a walk," he said and headed for the door.

He didn't ask me to join him, so I kept my place. It had been a difficult day for all of us. Uncle Edward had tried to keep the conversation going at dinner. He read the Christmas story, then blessed the food and added: "Lord, we thank thee for thy Son, Jesus, for his birth we celebrate today. We ask you to keep our loved ones safe and bring them home soon."

Everyone said "Amen." Even the boys from the air base. The ones from Easter had moved on, but there were always lonely men to take their place at Aunt Rose's table. These two were still in their teens. Too young for Mary Margaret to flirt with. She ate her meal in silence while Uncle Edward chatted with the boys.

Most of the conversation centered on the food. It was easy to see why. Aunt Rose must have saved her sugar ration for two months. There was apple pie and candied carrots, and sweet potatoes from the garden. Uncle Edward's cookies had bribed a turkey from the butcher, and we opened the last jar of homemade peach jam.

"I want the boys to have a meal to remember," Aunt Rose said. She didn't add, *Who knows when they'll get another?* but we all understood that's what she meant.

Jake was always uncomfortable around the airmen. Aunt Rose never failed to explain his background, and the boys thought of him as a hero. "You were on the *West Virginia?*" they would ask in awe. "Wow, that must have been something."

"Don't worry, sir," one of them had said today, "as soon as they turn us loose, we'll blast the stinkin' yellow bellies for ya. Sorry, ma'am." The boy turned red when he saw Aunt Rose's face and bowed his head over his plate, suddenly intent on a forkful of potatoes.

Uncle Edward quickly changed the subject, but I saw Jake stiffen, and the knuckles on his hand turned white as he clutched his fork.

The conversation died before the pie was gone, and the airmen left shortly after. Aunt Rose looked exhausted and waived me away when I started to clear the table. "We'll do this later, Cissy. Come sit awhile. We hardly get to visit as a family anymore."

That had been an hour ago, and we'd been sitting ever since, listening to Christmas records on the Victrola, everyone lost in his or her own thoughts.

I looked over at Mama in the wingback chair. Her head bobbed loosely to her shoulder. She lifted it once, then settled back into a restless sleep. I knew that so much company confused her.

She knew enough about the war to be afraid for Billy, but other ghosts haunted her as well. "What about Chuck?" she asked Jake and me one day. "If they let William join, will they take my Chuckie too?"

"Chuckie can't go, Mama, he's only twelve," I reminded her. But she worried just the same.

I studied the wrinkles on her hands, her snow-white hair and sunken cheeks. She and Aunt Rose were the same age; so why did Mama look so much older?

Jake was in the front yard flipping a football into the air and catching it. Uncle Edward watched him through the window. "How's he doing, Celia? Physically, I mean."

I thought a minute. "He's doing better. His arm is much stronger and the burns are healed. The doctors are amazed. He's still in pain though. He brushes it off, says it's nothing, but I can always tell when he uses that arm too much."

Aunt Rose stood and dabbed her damp eyes with a hankie. She was still a "handsome woman," as Uncle Edward called her, but her shiny auburn hair was showing flecks of gray. I noticed that the dress she'd worn three Christmases in a row hung a little loose this year.

"We'd best see to the kitchen," Aunt Rose sighed. "No, Cissy, you sit and talk to your uncle. Mary Margaret can help me with the dishes."

I saw a flicker of annoyance cross Mary Margaret's face. But instead of putting up a fuss like she would have done a month ago, she got up from the sofa and started clearing plates from the table.

"What's he going to do, Celia?" Uncle Edward coughed. "I'm sorry, sweetheart, I don't mean to pry. But if his arm is better, shouldn't he be looking for a job? You know, the offer is still open if he wants to come to work for me."

You can't support him forever. He didn't say it, but I knew that's what he meant. Everyone had been making comments lately—Mary Margaret, even Dotty.

"There's lots of openings at the factory."

I felt a flash of anger. "Shouldn't we get Mama home?" I saw the hurt on Uncle Edward's face and kissed him on the cheek. "Don't worry, Jake will find something soon. He just needs time, that's all."

But how much? I'd made up my mind to ask him several times in the last month or so, but circumstances were never right. *Maybe,* I thought, *it's because I don't want to hear the answer.*

Chapter
Twenty-six

Jake spent the first few chilly days of 1943 at the base with Chaplain Drain. I had no idea how they found so much to talk about, but Jake seemed happier somehow, even though he was sometimes up half the night rubbing his shoulder with Sloan's Liniment.

News of the war had escalated with more rumors of a vicious Navy, Air and Marine battle at Guadalcanal.

Jake wasn't surprised. "I told you we'd retake the islands. The sooner we clean up the Pacific, the sooner we'll win the war."

Sam nodded in agreement. "It won't be easy, though. We shouldn't underestimate this enemy. They're better trained and their men aren't afraid to die."

"And we send in a bunch of green recruits."

Jake was quoting from Wesley's latest letter. Mary Margaret had received it just a few days ago. It was dated August 6, 1942, and the pages were heavily blackened by the censor's marker.

"We'd be better off if they'd keep the children home and let us blow the _____ to smithereens."

He spoke of heavy rains and rough seas and "those wimps puking their guts out—stinking up the whole ship." One of the officers on board had to be hospitalized with a rash. "A nasty fungus—infected his entire body."

Wesley went on to say he'd been presented with his lieutenant bars. "About time too. I'm on a roll, kiddo. By the time this war is over, I'll be president! Ha Ha."

No words of love or "I miss you," but I think Mary Margaret had given up expecting any. "He has to come home someday. And we'll start over." But her voice sounded hollow when she said it.

Billy's letters were few and far between. One of us wrote to him at least once a week, Aunt Rose more often than that. But still he complained about not hearing from us.

"Gee, I hope you're all okay. I haven't gotten anything in two mail calls now. I wish I could send Christmas presents. I have money, but there's nowhere around here to buy anything." You could tell he'd tried to describe the weather and the scenery, but the censors had blacked most of it out.

"I don't see how Wesley got by with that 'fungus' thing." Jake sounded disgusted. "It's obvious they're both somewhere in the South Pacific."

He didn't say anything around Aunt Rose, of course. None of us did, but I think it was obvious even to her. She didn't talk about Billy much—just wrote to him faithfully. But I knew it tore her up when he didn't get her letters.

"He'll get them all at once, Rose Bud," Jake tried to tease her out of a blue mood. "Then he'll moan about how much time it takes to read them all!"

*　*　*

Two weeks into the new year the weather turned warmer. A bright poinsettia clung to the fence along the neighbor's driveway, and Aunt Rose said Captain Long's garden had started blooming again. The captain had actually been appointed as an adviser to the officers' staff at the naval base in Long Beach.

He'd taken a room not far from our apartment, and Aunt Rose had offered to tend his garden for him.

"I'm forever in your debt, dear lady. Please take all the blossoms you can use."

"He even bowed and kissed my hand. Can you imagine?" Aunt Rose actually giggled and turned red. But I knew she was pleased. And the garden gave her something else to turn her hands to. "I swear, Cissy, sometimes I feel so useless. There's a war going on," she said as if I didn't know. "I should be doing more."

I pointed out that she already did more than her share. She volunteered two afternoons at the Red Cross, and her Ladies Aid chapter rolled bandages and knitted socks for the boys in Europe.

"Our missions group is quilting blankets for the orphans in England," she said one day. "Do you have any fabric scraps, Cissy? We're starting another one Wednesday night after choir practice."

I just shook my head and handed her a bag of cotton material I'd been hoarding for a quilt of my own. "I'll never get around to it anyway," I told Jake later. "I'm glad Aunt Rose is staying busy, and if it keeps a child warm, that much the better."

Jake had been awfully quiet for the last few days. Still, he stayed busy around the apartment, and Friday night I came home to find dinner on the table.

I plucked a carnation from the centerpiece vase. "What's this?" I teased. "We celebrated our anniversary two weeks ago. Have you forgotten already?"

"Never."

He set a steaming plate of beans and wieners in the middle of the table, removed my apron from around his waist and danced me around the room.

"Jake Freeman, have you lost your mind? There isn't even

any music." I squealed as he flung me between his legs, spun around and grabbed my hands again.

"We'll make our own music." He laughed and pulled me close.

I closed my eyes and rested against his chest. His heart was pounding under my ear like a rubber drum, and it took me a minute to catch my breath.

He stood still, just holding me until our breathing slowed. I pushed back and looked up to see him smiling down at me.

"What is it?"

"I have news, babe. Great news. They're going to take me back."

* * *

"Arm or no arm, I can still do my part, Celia."

We were walking home from the grocer's two blocks from our apartment. Jake carried a sack of groceries in the crook of his left arm. The right one dangled at his side, where I knew he was clenching his fist and flexing his bicep, actions that had become second nature in the last few months. His face showed more animation than I'd seen in almost a year.

"This is too good an opportunity to pass up." He shifted the bag, and I steeled myself against reaching out to steady it. Jake had made it clear from the beginning that he didn't want my help.

It had taken Jake almost a month to realize he'd been given a general discharge instead of a medical one. "I guess I was just too mad to read it closely. Boy, am I glad you didn't let me burn those papers." He'd paced the floor last night like a rooster in a hen yard, too excited to sit, and talking so fast I couldn't get a word in edgewise.

Commander Drain had convinced a board of appeals that even though the three-month reenlistment time had expired, Jake's circumstances were unusual, and he would be an asset to the corps.

"Of course, it helps that they're short-handed at the yard. They needed a good mechanic and won't have to train me," Jake had yawned, kissed me good-night and fallen sound asleep.

Now, I tried to hide the fear that shot through me at the thought of his going back into the service. What if they shipped him out again? Then I felt guilty. This was what Jake wanted more than anything. How could I even think of spoiling his happiness?

I pushed back a lock of hair that the wind had blown into my eyes and prayed that the Lord would help me stay calm. "Are you sure?" I said quietly. "You still have so much pain. I thought the doctor said—"

"I'm going to do this, Cissy."

Jake only used my nickname to tease or as a form of endearment. I knew he'd said it that way to soften the blow. I also knew that nothing I could say would change my husband's mind.

Chapter
Twenty-seven

I will always think of February as a month of changes, of gloomy skies and foggy seas, long dark days and endless lonely nights. In February 1941, my bridegroom left to go to sea and came home a year later a broken man. Now, in February 1943, just when he'd begun to heal, he was leaving me again. I felt the Navy was a mistress I could not compete with.

"Don't worry, babe, I'll be fine. It's not like I'm headed for battle. I'm working in dry dock, remember?"

"On Oahu." I didn't add what I was thinking: *Oahu has been bombed before. What will stop it from happening again?*

Jake stood at the mirror, deftly fastening the buttons on his Navy blues. He slid the blouse over his head and reached for the tie. His eyes met mine in the glass. "Stop it," he said like he had read my mind. "That was a sneak attack. We're too well fortified now; they won't be back."

I threw off the covers and grabbed my robe from the foot of the bed. "I'm going with you to the station."

"No."

"Jake . . ."

He turned and knelt beside the bed. "Celia, we've been over this before. It's four a.m. and you have to get ready for work soon." He lowered me back onto my pillow. "Besides," his voice turned husky as he stroked my cheek, "I want to dream of you like this, lying warm and sleepy-eyed in my bed."

He kissed me gently, then stood and stared as if he wanted to memorize my face. "I'll be back, Cissy. This will all be over soon, and I'll be back before you even know I'm gone."

We both knew that was a lie.

* * *

Jake had been gone less than a month when I ran into Mr. Hyatt coming out of the elevator.

Uncle Edward had been by the night before to take Mary Margaret and me out to dinner. Gas was rationed and rubber for tires was scarce, so it was a real treat to have him come. "Rose has a guild meeting tonight, but she wanted you to have these." He handed us each a small bouquet of roses. "The first new blooms from Captain Long's garden."

That morning I picked out a beauty, a half-opened bloom of white, lacy petals trimmed in red. I wrapped it carefully in dampened newspaper and added a layer of dry, then stuck it in the milk-glass bud vase Dotty and Sam had given us for our second anniversary. I nearly dropped it getting off the bus, and I breathed a sigh of relief when I made it to the elevator with the bud intact.

When the doors opened on the second floor, I stepped into the reception hall right onto Mr. Hyatt's new Florsheims. He put his arms out to steady me, but it was too late. The vase tumbled onto the floor and landed in front of the water cooler.

"Well, Celia Summers!" He helped me regain my balance and walked over to retrieve the vase. "I'm afraid your bloom is spoiled, but the container seems to be in one piece." He handed me the vase. The bud drooped wearily from a broken stem. I checked the heavy milk-glass carefully, but it hadn't even cracked.

Then I noticed my boss's newly scuffed shoes. "Mr. Hyatt, I'm so sorry. I can't think why I didn't see you. Now I've ruined your shine."

I was still shaking when I got to my desk.

"He was the one blocking the doorway," Dotty pointed out. "You would think he'd know not to stand so close."

I took a deep breath and slid the empty vase into a drawer.

"He's sure been hanging around here a lot lately. You don't think he's spying on someone, do you?"

A chill crawled over my arms and up my neck.

Dotty must have seen my face. "Oh, Celia honey, I'm sorry. I didn't think."

"It's all right." I shook the feeling away. "I'm sure he's just up here on business. After all, he *is* a partner in the firm."

"Of course he is. It's just that he's never come around much before."

When we went on break at nine o'clock, Mr. Wildish was alone in his office and Hyatt was nowhere to be seen. At 9:20 we returned to find a huge bouquet of roses on my desk.

"What on earth?" Dotty grabbed them up and buried her face in the petals. "They're beautiful, Celia. Who do you suppose . . . ?"

A small white card fell to the carpet. I picked it up and read the two short lines aloud. "Mrs. Celia Freeman, I'm sorry about your flower. Robert Hyatt."

Only then did I remember that when the accident happened Mr. Hyatt had used my maiden name. I didn't say anything to Dotty for fear she'd mention it to Sam.

Mustn't resurrect old ghosts, I told myself. *He probably just saw it in my records.*

* * *

A week later, I'd forgotten all about the incident with the roses. Jake had written that all was well. He was working hard and enjoying Honolulu's balmy nights and sun-drenched days.

"It rains almost every day," he wrote, "gully washers that soak you to the skin. Then the sun comes out and even the sand is dry in half an hour.

"I wish you were here with me, babe. I miss you so much I could die."

"Why don't you go?" Dotty asked as we pushed through the doors after lunch. "You can find a typing job anywhere. It's not like Jake will be going out to sea. He might as well be a civilian with the duty he's got."

Because he's never asked me. And when I bring it up he hedges, like he knows something I don't know.

I kept my thoughts to myself and glanced at the desk behind mine. Still empty.

Everyone was buzzing with curiosity. Miss Kraus, the switchboard operator, had come into Mr. Wildish's office earlier that morning to inform him there was a call for Sara, one of the bookkeepers.

We weren't allowed to receive personal calls at Wildish and Hyatt. We weren't allowed to make them either except at lunch or break, and then only on the pay phone in the lobby. So when Miss Kraus came in and Wildish called Sara into his office, we knew it must be an emergency.

Sara came out of the office wide-eyed and terrified. "I-I'm needed at home," she stammered when someone asked her what was wrong. Then she grabbed her bag and ran through the double doors.

"She has a son at war," someone whispered.

Dotty reached across the aisle and grabbed my hand. *Lord, God, help her.* The page in my typewriter had blurred, and I'd been glad when the bell rang for lunch.

We hadn't been back ten minutes when Miss Kraus rushed in again, fumbling with the cord to her earphones. She kept her head down and burst right into the office without knocking.

"Great Scott, woman, what is it this time?"

The door banged shut, then opened again. Mr. Wildish looked flustered. He laid a hand on Miss Kraus's shoulder and nodded toward the entrance.

"Ah-hum." He cleared his throat and turned toward the room. "Mrs. Freeman, telephone for you. In my office, if you please."

I could hear Dotty's in-drawn breath. My heart stopped and I felt frozen to the chair.

Somehow I made it to the office. My hands shook so bad I could hardly hold up the receiver.

"Celia?"

The voice sounded small and far away. "This is Anne Marie. Ma's doing poorly, can you come?"

I swallowed the lump in my throat. "What is it, Annie? What's wrong with her?"

"She got a telegram. Oh, Cissy, our Timmy's dead."

Chapter
Twenty-eight

Jake's brother Tim had died in action on Eniwetok, on a patch of sun-scorched sand half a mile from the radio bunker he and his patrol were supposed to secure. We learned later that casualties from that battle had been light due to heavy shelling from our aircraft and ships before the Marines landed. But Tim and his buddies had been overcome on the first morning of a five-day battle against the suicidal Japanese defense.

They brought his body home a few weeks later and suggested we keep the flag-draped casket closed. Jake took emergency leave to come home for the funeral. He tried to explain war and dying to five trembling, white-faced children, but all they understood was "Timmy's not coming home anymore."

We did our best to comfort his mother and helped his father hang a gold star in the window. Jake and I cried for one night in each other's arms. Then he was gone again.

* * *

Mary Margaret finally heard from Wesley, and the censors had left all but one or two words alone. I wished they had blacked out the whole thing.

"You may be surprised to know I'm safe, just a bit waterlogged. That last battle was a ringer. We lost the _____. I don't know where I go from here, but I'm sure it won't be the States.

"Why wait for me, kiddo? It could be a long war, and when it's over there's a lot of world out there. I'm not sure I want to come home to a hick town like San Bernardino. If you want a divorce, I won't stop you."

"Maybe he's right, Celia. Maybe I should give it up."

Mary Margaret sat on the sofa and dabbed at her eyes with a hankie she'd retrieved from the pocket of her overalls. "Mother says I should stick with him and pray the Lord will change his heart. But I don't think even God can soften Wesley Harris."

She straightened up and ran a hand through her tangled curls. "Anyway, I'm sick to death of trying. It never was any good. Mother and Daddy were right. I never should have married him."

I didn't know what to say. Wesley was a cad, but he was Mary Margaret's husband—"for better or worse," the vows had said. And a divorce in our family would be worse than death.

Maybe he'll be killed in action. Shocked at my own thoughts, I turned my head away.

Mary Margaret stuck the letter in her pocket and stood. "I have to go, Celia. I need a hot bath."

Her eyes were red but dry as she headed for the door.

"Oh, I almost forgot." She turned, and we almost collided in the doorway. "I have to give up my room. Mrs. Williams is ill. She's selling the house and I have to be out by June. I thought maybe you and I . . . Well, now that Jake's gone . . ."

"You want to move in here?" I couldn't help but sound astonished.

"No, I just thought maybe this place was too big for you with Jake away. We could look at something smaller. Share the rent." Her voice rose with excitement as she talked. I thought of a child trying to convince her mother to buy her a new dress.

"We'll see." I hated the weakness in my voice.

"Just think about it, Celia. I don't need an answer for a week or two." She hurried down the hallway and disappeared around the bend in the stairs.

* * *

At first I thought it was just a coincidence when I kept bumping into Mr. Hyatt. Not literally, but he always seemed to be getting out of his car, a fancy Rolls Royce, when the bus dropped me off at work. It was the same every morning for a week. He'd send the driver on his way, then tip his hat and usher me through the doorway. When I left for home, he was either talking to the receptionist or handing out campaign buttons in the lobby.

"It's not just your imagination," Dotty agreed. "I've noticed it too. Everybody has." She must have seen the horror on my face. "Well, not exactly everybody. But face it, Celia, either the man's a lunatic or he's really stuck on you."

"Then he's a lunatic either way! I'm a married woman and he knows it."

Dotty frowned. "There is another possibility. I don't want to scare you, honey, but when I told Sam what Hyatt was doing, he said to tell you to be careful. He even suggested you call that detective friend of yours—what's his name?"

"Sergeant Harman? He's no friend of mine and you know it! He'd probably side with Hyatt. Anyway," I added, trying to sound casual, "Mr. Hyatt hasn't actually done a thing. I'm sure it's all just a coincidence."

Dotty didn't look convinced. "Just be careful, Celia. Look what those creeps did to Sam."

I shuddered. "Those creeps are in prison," I assured her. But I wasn't convinced myself.

* * *

Two days later, I had just pulled a letter from Jake out of my mailbox when I heard voices. I looked up and saw Mr. Hyatt talking with the manager of my apartment building.

"Why, there she is now. Yoo-hoo, Celia, this gentleman's been inquiring for you."

Hyatt looked disconcerted, and I had no choice but to acknowledge his greeting and hope Mrs. Dillon wouldn't go back inside.

She didn't disappoint me.

"You look like a lady who could use a good meal. Will you join me for dinner, Mrs. Freeman? I'd like to talk to you."

Mrs. Dillon scowled and took a step backward into her apartment, but I noticed she didn't shut the door.

"I c-can't, sir. My uncle will be here any minute; we're going to the movies." A lame excuse, but at least it sounded plausible.

"Well, another time then." He tipped his hat, but made no move to leave.

From somewhere I found the courage to speak. "Mr. Hyatt, have we met before?" His eyes narrowed, and I forced myself to continue. "You do look familiar, and the other day you called me Miss Summers." I wondered if it sounded like the challenge I meant it to be, but he seemed to relax.

"As a matter of fact, that's why I wanted to talk to you. I knew your father some time ago; we had business dealings, and I recognized you from a picture he showed me." He hesitated, then added, "I heard he'd gone to prison. I trust everything is all right now?"

He looked genuinely concerned, but I couldn't help but feel uneasy. "My father is dead, Mr. Hyatt." It crossed my mind that if they were friends, he should have known. At any rate, it was all over the news.

"I am sorry." He pulled a small gold watch out of his pocket and examined it carefully. "Well, I must go. I have a campaign speech in less than an hour. Take care, Mrs. Freeman."

He pushed his way out the doors just as the silver Rolls slid up to the curb. When they pulled away, I began to breathe again.

Mrs. Dillon came back into the hallway. "What an odd man." She touched my arm. "If you need me, dear, you know where I am."

*   *   *

Uncle Edward was alarmed when I told him about Mr. Hyatt's strange behavior. "You can't stay alone there, Celia; I won't have it."

He'd already called Sergeant Harman, who as I expected put the whole thing down to "a man looking for a date." That's how Uncle Edward put it, but I could tell by the way he hesitated that the detective had used other words. "Tell her to hose him down next time. That ought to cool his *amour*."

"You should come home to us," Aunt Rose had insisted. "And Mary Margaret too. It's not safe for either of you to be alone."

"I won't go home, Celia," Mary Margaret confided later. "I need my job at Douglas. And you need yours. Besides, I want some independence."

I sighed. Mary Margaret was right. "All right, you win. We'll get a place together."

Uncle Edward finally agreed. "I won't tell Jake about your boss, not this time. But you girls be careful."

I *was* careful. For weeks I never went anywhere in the building alone, and I made sure Elmer, the elevator man, was at his post before I got on. I kept my head down when Mr. Hyatt was in the office so I wouldn't have to look at him.

Dotty looked, though. She watched him like a hen stalking a worm, giving him the evil eye any chance she had.

"Stop it!" I elbowed her one day when she glared him out of the office. "Don't lose your job over this, Dot. It's not worth it."

"Yes it is," she grinned. "Besides, he and Mr. Wildish have been on the outs lately, and Wildish likes me." She giggled and stuck a wad of gum in her mouth. "Ever since he and Miss Kraus started getting friendly, they both treat me like a daughter."

The picture of Dotty standing shoulder to shoulder with Miss Kraus and Mr. Wildish in a family portrait flashed through my mind, and I laughed out loud. Luckily, the bell rang for lunch, and I just gave Mr. Wildish my prettiest smile when he stuck his head through the office door.

"Have a nice lunch, ladies," he said.

Dotty winked at him as we walked by, and I nearly tripped over the edge of the carpet trying to escape.

We were as giddy as schoolgirls that day, although I can't think why. Maybe it was the weather—sunny and hot enough to get a tan with your clothes on.

Or maybe it was because classes were over for Sam, for this year anyway. He'd found a great summer job as an apprentice to the law school dean. He'd actually been doing that all year, but this would be full time and, like Dot said, would fatten his bankbook a bit.

And maybe hasten a proposal, I thought.

I had an apple and a bologna sandwich for lunch. The clock on the wall in the cafeteria said twelve-thirty.

"We've got a half hour left," I said. "I'm going to run over to Woolworth's and get some stationery. I ran out last night, and I want to write to Jake."

Dotty folded up the letter she'd been reading and stuck it in her bag. "I'll go with you."

I knew her mother had just sent her a stack of mail from her uncle and a brother in Europe. I also knew she was dying to finish reading them, so I waved her back.

"Don't be silly. You stay. I'll only be a few minutes, and it's just down the block." She looked hesitant, so I pointed to the chair. "Sit. It's broad daylight. I'll be fine."

She sat, and I hurried from the room before she could change her mind.

Chapter
Twenty-nine

I suppose I shouldn't have gone into the alley. But, looking back, I know a confrontation was inevitable.

It only took ten minutes at Woolworth's to buy a tablet of note paper and some envelopes. Our offices were in the middle of the block, and I had plenty of time to get back to work. So when the tiger cat trotted past me with a kitten in her mouth and turned down the alley, I decided to follow.

You can't have a cat, Celia Freeman, your apartment is too small. But what if she has a whole litter that needs rescuing?

The debate with myself took me halfway down the alley, where the cat paused, looked at me as if to say, *Come see my babies,* and disappeared behind a group of metal trash cans. She had made a nest clear in the back, behind an apple box. I could hear the frantic mewing of hungry kittens and see the mother's tail twitch as she settled herself around them for their afternoon meal.

I moved one of the containers aside slowly so as not to scare them and got down on my haunches for a better look. There were six babies with their eyes open, fat and healthy-looking just like their mama. *She belongs to someone,* I assured myself and decided the mama cat could manage on her own.

Getting out of my position wasn't as easy as getting in there. I lost my balance when I tried to turn around. Before I could catch myself, I felt two gloved hands grab my elbows and lift me to my feet.

My mind registered a rather short man in a dark overcoat, with black leather gloves and a black wide-brimmed hat pulled down over his eyes. An odor of stale smoke and gasoline made my stomach lurch. Before I could blink, his grip moved from my elbows to my neck, and I gasped for air as his thumbs pressed against my throat.

I grabbed his wrists. They were small, but strong as steel, and I couldn't break his hold. Spots of black and yellow light bounced behind my eyes, and I felt the world dissolve around me, like being lost in a cold dark cave.

Then he let me go. I fell to my knees, scraping my hands across the gravel, and fought to draw air into my burning lungs. It felt like hours, but I guess it was only seconds later that the roaring in my ears subsided. I heard a voice and the sound of square-heel shoes clunking down the alley.

"Oh, my stars! Celia, are you all right?" Miss Kraus hurried toward me. Her spectacles dangled from a string of yellow yarn around her neck and bounced against the hand she held clutched to her heart. "I saw the whole thing. That horrid man!"

By the time I could speak again, Dotty was there along with several others from the second floor. They helped me into the building. Miss Kraus had just phoned the police when Mr. Wildish and Mr. Hyatt stepped off the elevator and hurried to my side.

* * *

I had stopped shaking by the time we got back to my apartment. A blessed numbness had settled over my mind, but my head throbbed and it was hard to swallow. The doctor had given me some salve for my scraped hands and assured me the bruises on my throat would heal in about a week.

Dotty grabbed a glass from the cupboard, filled it with water from the tap and handed me one of the pills the doctor had prescribed. "It burns me up that the police haven't caught that guy. How could he disappear just like that? And that horrible lieutenant . . . !"

I flushed when I remembered the probing, the smirks on the faces of the two policemen who had questioned me at the hospital. "Probably a lovers' quarrel," I had heard one of them say on the way out the door.

Dotty snorted. "Miss Kraus didn't help the situation. She only saw him from behind and told the police it looked like he was trying to force his advances on you."

I sank into the sofa and groaned as Dotty tried to massage the soreness from my temples.

"I'm sleeping here tonight. And don't argue." She pushed my shoulders back down. "There's no way you're staying here alone."

"Oh, Dot, how would I survive without you? You and Sam give me so much support. With Jake gone . . ."

I let the sentence trail off. With Jake in Oahu, I felt so alone. Uncle Edward and Aunt Rose were so far away.

"We'll phone your uncle in the morning."

I knew she was right, but I dreaded telling them. It would worry them to death.

*　*　*

Chaplain Drain showed up just as Dotty was leaving the next morning. After greeting her he handed me a box of chocolates and a single red rose. "From Jake," he said. "I promised to deliver them myself. Besides, I wanted to see how you were getting along, especially since I feel responsible for your husband being gone."

I smiled, took the flower and motioned him into the living

room. "Jake was miserable, commander. If you hadn't helped him get back into the service, I don't know what he would have done."

The bruises on my neck had already faded to a tinge of yellow, but the chaplin noticed right away.

"Excuse me for saying this, Celia, but you look ill. Is there anything I can do?"

He proved to be as good a listener with me as he had been with Jake, and I found myself telling him the whole story.

"The police think it was just a random incident, but what if it is connected with my father and the attack on Sam and me? Dotty thinks I should quit my job at Wildish and Hyatt. Whoever this character is, he knows where I work, and she's afraid he might try again. So," I grimaced and passed him the opened box of candy, "if you know anyone who needs a secretary . . ."

He looked thoughtful. "You know, I just might. I'll let you know this afternoon."

He stood and moved toward the door. "Are you sure you want to stay here alone? I'd be happy to run you out to your uncle's place."

I shook my head. "No, commander, but thank you. Uncle Edward is coming for me this evening. I'll be fine till then."

Mrs. Dillon's head popped out of her apartment doorway when I walked the commander downstairs. "Don't worry, I'm safe here," I said again as I let him out of the building. I smiled at her furrowed brow and knew it was true.

* * *

I set a glass of milk in front of Uncle Edward and handed him a fork for his cake. Aunt Rose had managed, as usual, to serve a full meal in spite of the rationing.

Uncle Edward patted my hand. He'd already contacted Sergeant Harman and delivered him a lecture that made the rafters rattle. Aunt Rose's dinner had calmed him some, but he still wore a worried frown.

"Celia, what we said before still goes. You're welcome to come home anytime. But as long as you're on your own, please be careful. You've been protected so far, but you have to use your head." He gripped my hand and made me look into his eyes. "No more alleys, Celia. Do you understand?"

I nodded soberly. "No more alleys. I promise to be more careful." He didn't look satisfied, but Aunt Rose changed the subject.

"What about this job with Captain Long?"

Uncle Edward smiled. "I have to hand it to the captain; his timing couldn't have been better. Although . . . I have a feeling the chaplain had something to do with it."

"I'm sure of it," I said, remembering the phone call I'd received less than an hour after Commander Drain had left my apartment. "But I probably should be heading back. Captain Long wants me in his office 'by 0900 hours' tomorrow."

"Finish your dessert, sweetheart. Edward will run you home in the morning, won't you dear?"

Uncle Edward folded his napkin and pushed back from the table. "We'd better head for bed then. We'll need to leave early."

*　*　*

Captain Long greeted me and settled himself nimbly behind his desk. "Silly old woman," he mumbled. "Thinks she can retire in the middle of a war. A lot of good years left in her too. Ahhum," he said, catching himself, "you don't want to hear this nonsense, now do you?" The captain straightened a stack of papers that were perfectly straight to begin with, and I had to stifle a smile.

"Thing is, my dear, I need a secretary. That is to say, *we* need a secretary." He glanced across the hallway where Chaplain Drain sat at his desk behind a glass partition. He was talking on the phone but smiled and waved when he saw us looking his direction. "The good chaplain often has letters to dictate, and I'm a busy man. Can't expect me to type my own correspondence now, can they?

"But what am I to do?" he asked. "I've three letters and a report overdue, and that confounded woman just walks away. Well? What do you say, girl? It's only part time, of course, but you can start tomorrow."

"That's very kind of you, captain, but are you sure? I mean, can you hire a civilian?"

"My dear girl, of course I can. I can hire anyone I please. It's done, then. Tomorrow morning, 0800 sharp." He stood and took my hand. I thought he wanted to shake hands, like a gentleman closing a business deal, but he held it in his palm instead and patted it absently while opening the door.

I felt like a little girl being dismissed by a loving father. "I love you, Cissy," I heard Papa say, "I really do."

"We love you, sweetheart," Uncle Edward had said the night before. "You know we'll always be here when you need us."

Chapter
Thirty

My head was still whirling a week later. I had managed to catch up on the captain's correspondence, but it was obvious they didn't need me every day. So when Mr. Wildish offered me a substantial raise to come back to the firm for four days a week, I agreed.

"You're the best typist they have and they know it," Dotty said when I saw her that weekend. "I still think it's risky, but boy did I miss you!" She grinned and put her arm around my shoulders. "I'm glad you're back, but what about the captain?"

I thought about the empty in-box on my desk in the captain's office and smiled. "Both the captain and the commander have decided I can handle things just fine on Friday afternoons."

"And the tyrants have agreed to let you work four days a week?" She shook her head and handed me a carrot. "Be a doll and chop this into the salad, will you? Sam will be here in ten minutes, and dinner's not even on the stove."

While we got things ready for dinner, Dotty filled me in on all the happenings at the office while I was away. "Mr. Hyatt upped security outside the building. He says, if you were attacked what's to stop someone from trying to assassinate him? Can you imagine? As if he were that important."

I reached for a stalk of celery. "The last I heard, he had a good chance to win." Somehow the thought of Robert Hyatt becoming my congressman made me feel ill.

". . . and Wildish won't let Miss Kraus out of his sight," Dotty went on like I hadn't said a word. "They're getting pretty thick. But when Hyatt asked Mr. Wildish about it, he told him to mind his own business and start doing his share of work. We weren't supposed to hear, of course, but their voices were so loud, the entire second floor was on alert!

"And then," she giggled and turned the flame down under the green beans, "then, the very next day Hyatt caught Mr. Wildish kissing Miss Kraus in the elevator! I wasn't there, but Ella was standing right behind Mr. Hyatt. She said the doors opened and there they were!"

"Quit the gossip, you two, or I'm going back to my books."

Neither of us had heard Sam come into the room. Dotty screeched and slapped her hand to her chest, and I nearly dropped the salad bowl.

Sam grinned. "I oiled the wheels last night. You two cats wouldn't have heard me anyway. Want me to go home and fetch some cream?"

Dotty stuck her tongue out, then bent and kissed him on the cheek. I felt a flutter of envy, but pushed it aside. At least Jake and I were man and wife. I knew Sam loved Dotty, but he still wouldn't declare himself.

"Sam is smart," Jake had told me once. "He'll make a darn good lawyer, but school and study take up all his time, not to mention money. He'll ask Dot to marry him when he knows he can support her."

"But Dotty would help him, Jake," I'd insisted. "She makes enough to support them while he tends to school."

Jake shook his head and flashed a look I couldn't read. "You don't understand, Celia."

He was right. I didn't.

Neither did Dot, but she was patient, I'll give her that. "Samuel Levi is the only man I want," she insisted when I asked her why she didn't date someone else. "I'll wait forever if I have to."

Sam took the wooden bowl from me, grabbed the tongs off the counter and wheeled them smoothly to the table. The muscles on his upper arms rippled under his shirt as he lifted a ladder-backed chair out of the way. It never ceased to amaze me how strong Sam's upper body was. He worked out with weights every day, even while studying.

Dotty had confided that he'd fired his nurse months ago. "I couldn't stand to have that female fussing over me like I was a two-year-old," he'd told her. "I'll do fine on my own. Besides, you're right next door. All I have to do is bang on the wall."

"I wish I was closer than next door," she told me wistfully. All I could do was smile and squeeze her hand.

* * *

Mary Margaret and I took a six-month lease on a small apartment at the corner of Cherry and Beverly Way in Long Beach. The three small rooms were cramped and stuffy, even on the best of days.

I had tried to persuade her to look at some other places, but she wouldn't hear of it. "It won't matter," she insisted and pulled out her checkbook. "We spend most of our time at work. Anyway, this is closer for both of us."

I'd given in as usual. Besides, she was right. The Douglas plant was only a few blocks away, and the naval base an easy ten-minute bus ride. But no matter how much she protested, I knew she really wanted to be near the harbor, in case Wesley's ship should pull in and he should decide to come home.

You wouldn't know it to hear her talk, though. "I'm through trying, Celia," she'd say. "There's no sense in beating a dead horse. If Wesley doesn't love me, nothing I do will change his mind."

She wrote him almost every day.

* * *

In late September, I spent one night with Jake on Oahu. This time it was Captain Long who pulled the strings.

September had been hotter than June, July and August put together. Mary Margaret and I had spent the weekend helping Aunt Rose and Uncle Edward in the garden. By Saturday night we'd consumed at least a gallon of Aunt Rose's lemonade. I was exhausted, and Mary Margaret had a sunburn. She'd refused Aunt Rose's offer of a hat.

"I don't need that, Mother. I've been to the beach a thousand times this summer—I'm used to the sun."

Now she was paying for her stubbornness.

"Hold still." I clenched my jaw as she squealed and pulled away from the vinegar rag I was trying to apply to the back of her neck. "I know it hurts, but this will draw the heat. You'll feel better in a few minutes."

"Ouch! Oh, Celia, my head is throbbing. How could I know the sun would be that strong?"

"Because your mother told you it would," I snapped. "But then, why would you listen to her? You never have before."

We were in our old room, Mary Margaret lying face down on her bed with me straddling her back. The skin from her neck to the edge of her halter top was a dark vermillion and had already started sprouting blisters. The bowl of vinegar water was balanced precariously on the bed beside us. I soaked the rag, wrung it out and laid it gently over the burn. It took only seconds for the rag to get hot, and I had to reapply the poultice again and again for any cooling effect.

"Owwww. That hurt! Celia, what's wrong with you?"

"I'm tired." I realized my patience had grown thin and my

prudence with it. I'd spent an entire summer listening to Mary Margaret whine. There were times when I couldn't blame Wesley for wanting to stay away.

I sighed and wrung the rag out one more time. "You know I love you," I said, laying it gently across her shoulders. "You've always been like a sister to me. But you're twenty-three years old. You need to grow up a little."

Her body stiffened, and she turned her face into the pillow. When she came up for air, her eyes were closed, her reddened cheeks bright with tears. "I can't grow up, Cissy; it hurts too bad."

Uncle Edward knocked on the door a few minutes later and invited us to go to the movies.

"Shh," I said, getting up and shutting the door quietly behind me. "She's asleep."

He was instantly contrite. "Is the sunburn bad?"

I nodded. "Bad enough. But she'll be fine in a few days. I don't think she'll be up for church tomorrow, though. Or work on Monday, unless it gets better fast."

"Maybe we should stay home, then."

Aunt Rose came up behind him. "No, Edward, you and Cissy go. I'll stay with Mary Margaret."

"Why don't all of you go so I can get some sleep?" Mary Margaret's voice was foggy with the laudanum Aunt Rose had given her earlier.

I really wanted nothing but a cool bath and a long nap. But it was still early and much too hot to sleep.

I found the movie boring but watched the newsreels closely for any sign of Billy or Wesley. We all knew the chances of seeing them were next to zero, but Uncle Edward would always study the films, then compare them to Billy's letters home. Much later we would learn that his and Jake's predictions about Billy's whereabouts were usually accurate.

Lately there had been a change in those letters. They were stiffer, less emotional. Oh, he still complained about the food. This last time he'd assured us, "If I see one more can of Spam, I'm going to set it on a stump and use it for target practice!" But he'd learned to be more careful with his words, and the censor marks were not as frequent as before.

"He's growing up," Uncle Edward said when Aunt Rose commented on the change. But I knew it was more than that. There was an underlying sadness in his words. Regret that he'd put himself in such a spot? He was just seventeen, he could still be home dancing with a high-school sweetheart or playing softball at the park. But, although he vowed he loved and missed us, "especially Mom's home cooking," he never whined or admitted he'd made a mistake.

He did seem restless, though. "We haven't seen the enemy in weeks," he complained in a letter dated June 16, 1943. "Unless you count the insects and the poisonous snakes. Rumor has it we'll be on the move again _____ . Maybe we'll see more action then."

Chapter
Thirty-one

Mary Margaret opened the front door as soon as we pulled into the drive. She was wrapped in the silk flowered robe Wesley had sent her for Christmas, shivering in spite of the heat.

Aunt Rose's face turned pale. "What is it? What's wrong?"

The skin on Mary Margaret's face was taut and red. She winced as she waved aside her mother's concern. "I'm sure it's nothing." She turned to me. "Jake called. He said to tell you to contact Captain Long tonight. He said it's important."

I looked at the clock. "It's so late. Did he say why?" I hated the feeling—half-nausea, half pain—that crept from my stomach into my throat. The fact that Jake himself had called should have assured me he was well, but my hands still shook as I dialed the captain's number.

"Don't be preposterous, girl, I don't have time to sleep." He seemed offended that I'd apologized for waking him. "Dashed inconvenient that you're in San Berdo. Can your uncle drive you up tonight? We have to be off at first light. Long flight, you know."

I felt my face flush with excitement. "Long flight? To where, sir? Where are we going?"

"To Oahu, of course. Didn't that scamp Jake tell you anything? I'll box his ears for you later. Now get back here and get packed. Just a small bag, you understand, we're only going overnight, and I don't have room for any female finery or doodads."

* * *

Years later, I would return to the island under calmer circumstances. I would fly over Pearl Harbor, visit the memorial and cry buckets of tears. Then I would move on to Maui, bake my body on sun-warmed beaches and play in the emerald waters with the rest of the tourists.

This time though, the captain's plane dipped down without fanfare, and I barely had time to breathe in the flower-scented air before we were hustled to a waiting limousine. My view of the island was limited to what I could see through the windshield; all the other windows were draped with ink-black shades.

The car stopped just inside the entrance to the base. I clutched the captain's arm as he gallantly led me past gawking sailors. I tried to ignore the whistles and catcalls that accompanied us to the visitors' waiting room.

The captain stopped a few feet short of the entrance, and I found myself caught up in my husband's embrace. Instead of the private meeting I'd envisioned on the long flight over, we were center stage for a performance that I'm sure kept its audience entertained for days.

"Wa-hooo!" Jake lifted me off my feet, spun me around till I felt dizzy, then kissed me long and hard without so much as a thought to the cheers and applause that erupted around us.

The last thing I remember before my husband bowed to the crowd and led me away was the dignified Captain Long, head thrown back, laughing uproariously and clapping with the rest of the men.

* * *

"I'm sorry, babe, I know this is a blow to you, but it's out of my control."

Jake had ordered in rice and chicken for our supper. I pushed my plate away and concentrated on my husband's feet as he paced back and forth across the tiny hotel room. Candlelight cast flickering shadows on the blackened windows. The wine, compliments of the captain, tasted bitter in my mouth.

He sat back down, reached across the table and captured my hands. I hadn't realized how much they were shaking until he tried to hold them still. His eyes bored holes in mine, pleading for understanding, asking me to be brave.

My mouth felt dry and my eyes stung, like I'd been running face first into a desert wind. "When?" I finally said.

He looked away. "Tomorrow, Celia. I leave tomorrow right after you do." He came around the table and pulled me to my feet. "Please, let's not waste our time together fighting. I'm just so glad to see you. If it weren't for Captain Long . . ."

I nodded. "I'm grateful, Jake, I really am. It's just . . . I didn't think you'd ever go back out to sea." My vision blurred, and I fought to control the tremor in my voice. "It's selfish, I know, but I'd hoped you'd finish out the war here, in dry dock. At least it's close to home." I pressed my face against his chest and felt his fingers, feather-light, run through my hair.

He kissed my forehead. I drew a deep breath and sat down on the edge of the bed. "Tell me about the ship."

His eyes brightened instantly. "The *Appalachian* is a brand-new flag ship, assigned to Rear Admiral Conolly. I'll be there for the christening in a week or so. The captain, Fernald I think his name is, said they needed a crack mechanic, and Commander Watts recommended me." He was pacing again, this time with excitement and enthusiasm for his new adventure.

"What about—?"

"My arm?" He turned to face me. "It's fine. I mean, it hurts, sometimes more than others, but I can do my job." He came and knelt beside the bed, his hands on my knees, his voice low and gravely with emotion. "This is an honor, Cissy. A year ago I thought my life was wasted. I felt useless and afraid. The chaplain gave me courage to believe in myself again. He convinced me that my life had a purpose. This is God's will, Celia. This is where I'm supposed to be." He stroked my cheek and looked at me, his eyes soft with wonder and peace.

Why, his faith is stronger than mine. I realized I had a lot of praying to do.

* * *

I propped my back against a wooden piling and let the government-issue binoculars fall against my chest. Our landlady's brother was down with the flu, and I had volunteered to stand his watch as air-raid warden for a couple days.

Fog roamed the pier in shifting pockets, veiling any hint of sunrise and obstructing my view of the early-morning sky. It wasn't likely there would be any war planes. There hadn't been a sighting since Pearl Harbor—at least, none here in Long Beach. Still, we couldn't be too careful. No one thought Hawaii would be attacked either, and look what came of that.

I rubbed my aching eyes and let my gaze focus on the old man and little boy. They'd been fishing from the end of the pier for over an hour now, reeling in mackerel like a couple of starving seals. It wasn't yet seven; they were violating curfew, but I didn't have the heart to send them away.

My wool sweater felt scratchy as I pulled it tighter around me. It was late October 1943. The weather had turned nippy almost overnight, and a sweater wasn't near enough protection from the morning chill.

Just as I'd convinced myself to turn and go, the man hauled in a small sand shark.

I hadn't heard such whooping and hollering since Billy

turned loose a garden snake in Aunt Rose's kitchen. That was years ago, but the memory of it made me want to laugh out loud. Tarzan, my fat old tomcat, was a spry young hunter then. He had that snake fairly flying across Aunt Rose's linoleum. By the time Billy realized he'd made a mistake, his old Labrador, Colby, decided to get in on the fun too.

Colby and Tarzan worked like a team and got the snake trapped between them. But just as they pounced in for the kill, their prey managed to slither through a small hole into the pan drawer at the bottom of the stove.

When Aunt Rose and Mary Margaret came running to see what all the ruckus was about, Billy took off out the back door. Before I could sputter, "S-s-snake," from my perch on top of the kitchen table, Aunt Rose shooed the animals away and yanked open the drawer.

The snake must have been paralyzed with fear. When Tarzan leaped over Aunt Rose's head into the drawer, it didn't even wiggle. But Colby wasn't about to give up the prize. He and Tarzan neatly split their catch, and the snake became the blue-plate special right there on the kitchen floor.

Poor Aunt Rose. Her face went pale as a whitewashed fence. Mary Margaret knocked her over trying to make it to the bath-room, and Colby chose that instant to decide he didn't like snake after all.

Now Colby had died, and Billy was fending off poisonous snakes somewhere in the South Pacific.

The little boy whooped again as his grandfather cut his line and booted the flapping shark back into the water.

The fog lifted, and the wooden planks began to steam in the sun. I stood and watched as the old man put away his pole, picked up their string of fish and grabbed the young boy's hand.

"Do we got enough for breakfast, Grandpa?" The child's eyes still danced from the fun with the shark.

The man nodded, looking up at me, then down at the boy. "We do, Jacob. Enough for you and me, and Mom and Grandma too."

I know he saw my ID band, but he must have realized I wouldn't scold them and smiled pleasantly in my direction as they shuffled by.

"I got a fish, missus, see? Isn't it a beaut?"

My heart caught the little one's smile and held it fast. I must have managed an answer, because the boy raced after his grandfather, eyes beaming with delight.

"They're all that's left," I thought as a wave of self-pity buffeted my spirit. "Old men and little boys. All the young men are at war."

The sun warmed the pier and weakened my resolve to go home. I slid down the piling and closed my eyes. Somewhere a band struck up the national anthem. The sad-sweet bugle notes died away and were replaced by a Tommy Dorsey rendition of "Harbor Lights" wafting from someone's radio. I tried to close out the sound. Since Jake had gone back to sea, I couldn't bear the lyrics to that song.

A flock of raucous gulls invaded the pier and squabbled over the few scraps of bait the old man had left behind. Suddenly I felt weary beyond belief. I pushed to my feet and grabbed the piling. The ripples of nausea that had been lapping at my stomach all morning surged into a teeming wave, and I leaned out over the railing.

When the sickness subsided, I thought of Mama. How she'd rush into the bathroom morning after morning and take to her bed in the afternoon.

I shook my head. It couldn't be. Jake and I had been together only once in the last nine months—in Hawaii, the day before he'd left for New York and the *Appalachian.* That was almost five weeks ago, and I hadn't heard from him since.

A whistle blared, announcing the shift change at Douglas. If I didn't hurry, Mary Margaret would beat me home and I'd be late for work. She liked a good long soak after a night on the line. I couldn't blame her, but I needed to shower and catch the eight-forty bus.

Chapter
Thirty-two

Dear Mom and Dad, I hope everything's all right at home. We have mail call every week now, but not everyone gets a letter. It's okay, though, I'm sure I'll get a dozen from you all at once.

"Things are pretty crazy here. My buddy Craig got a fever. He died last night. How can somebody die from a fever in the war? It doesn't make sense to me, but it sure got me thinking about why God lets things happen like they do.

"Most of the guys know I believe in God. I get teased a lot, but they always ask me to pray before we go on patrol. Can't blame them; every day someone kills a _____. This morning I shook a spider the size of an avocado pit out of my boot. The air smells like a garbage dump and everything's poisonous, including the mosquitoes, which is what they say killed Craig.

"I guess this must be the longest letter I've ever written. Maybe the sergeant will get tired of reading and let the whole thing go through. How about it, sarge?

"Well I just wanted to tell you I'm okay. Please write soon.

"Your Loving Son, Billy

"P.S. I'm even on a baseball team. The sergeant is as old as Dad, but boy can he throw a mean curve!"

* * *

By the first of December I knew it was true. "I'm pregnant, Aunt Rose."

Aunt Rose smiled and set aside the pan of dried apricots and cherries she was dicing for a fruitcake. She had already mixed the batter and chopped the nuts and dates into the large mixing bowl.

"I thought you might be." She hugged me and placed her hand against my still-flat belly. "Have you been to the doctor? Do you know when . . . ?"

I shook my head. "Not yet. I see the Navy doctor next Tuesday. But as close as I can figure, sometime in late June or early July."

She sighed and touched my cheek. "I'm happy for you. Babies are so sweet, and children can be such a blessing." She stared out the window, where a flock of chickadees were plucking seeds and insects from the empty garden.

"I hope Jake will be here," I went on to distract her. "He may get home for Christmas, did I tell you?"

"No. How wonderful! And of course he'll be here when the baby's born. The war can't possibly last that much longer." She ran her sticky fingers under the tap and dried them on a tea towel.

"Are you going to tell your mother? She'll be thrilled, I'm sure."

"If she understands. I think I'll wait until it's obvious." I tied on an apron and began to set the table for dinner.

Mama had been spending more and more time in bed, and her memory seemed worse than ever. The doctor said she may have had a stroke, although she showed no other signs.

The head nurse had tried to be reassuring. "She can move around and communicate when she wants to. It's my opinion she just doesn't want to bother. Get her to take a walk with you, or sit out on the patio and talk. A shawl will do if the weather's cool. She's a lot stronger than she looks."

* * *

December 7 came and went. We all tried to ignore the implications of that day, but it was hard when the radio and newsreels rehashed the whole event. It was hard to believe two years had gone by—two years of waiting, worrying, suffering and death.

Billy hadn't made it home all this time. "I have lots of leave built up and nowhere to go. We can't come home to the good old USA, and there aren't any towns nearby."

Yet news from Europe and the Pacific was encouraging. The war seemed to be going in our favor on all fronts, although it was rumored that Hitler was becoming more and more vicious, massacring innocent people, especially Jews, whom he insisted were nothing more than chattel, nonhumans, a detriment to the "pure" race.

Of course, we all hoped it wasn't true. We'd heard of "that madman" and his atrocities for years. Most of our leaders insisted the reports were exaggerated. Still, if even half of what they said was true . . . I shuddered. It was too horrible to contemplate.

I knew the reports bothered Sam terribly. He would go quiet and stiff as stone, then wheel his chair into another room, and we wouldn't see him for the rest of the evening. "He won't talk about it," Dotty said after we heard one particularly vicious rumor about a place called Auschwitz, in Poland. "His mother thinks their cousins are safe in Palestine, but no one has heard from them in months. I know Sam's angry, and he has a right to be, but he has some silly notion that if his legs were stronger he could do something for them. As if anyone can."

"Surely there's some way to find them."

"He's tried, Celia. Believe me, he's tried everything except go over there himself."

* * *

Jake's last letter had come in mid-November. He said that they were headed for the Pacific, but he didn't know where they would go from there. "Rumor has it we're bringing Admiral Conolly aboard in San Diego. Wouldn't it be great if I could get home for Christmas? Don't count on it though, babe. Chances are we'll be gone again by then. Even if we aren't, liberty is hard to come by. I'll let you know as soon as I do."

I tried not to get my hopes up, but I didn't tell him about the baby, just in case. "I want to be with him when he finds out," I told Mary Margaret. "And if he doesn't get home, I can send a telegram. I'll know more then anyway.

"I hope it comes before the weather gets too hot. Sally Davis nearly died when she had to carry her baby all through July. She was big as a house and had an awful time."

Mary Margaret shuddered and studied my stomach like it was about to sprout horns. "I don't know, Celia. I don't think it's worth it."

I laughed and splashed her with water from the sprinkle bowl I was using as I ironed a blouse for work the next day. A cool breeze flowed through the open window, and I was glad for the relief that evening brought. The nausea and dizziness that struck me every morning were gone by three or four o'clock. But I could see why Mama had been so miserable with Chuckie and Grace and, of course, the baby that died.

I pushed those thoughts away. I prayed all the time that Chuckie and Grace were safe and happy. We had no reason to think otherwise. If we could go by what I saw at St. Stephen's the day they took them away, the people who adopted them were well-to-do and could give them a better life than we ever could.

Not that Uncle Edward wouldn't have done it. He tried so many times to find them. Finally Mama, in one of her more lucid moments, told him to leave it be.

"They're better off where they are, Edward. You have your hands full with Cissy and your own two, not to mention that you've taken me on as well. The agency assured me they would have a good Christian upbringing, and that's all I ever wanted for any of my children." She had started to cry then, and Uncle Edward never brought up the subject again. At least not with Mama.

Mary Margaret picked up a book and headed toward the bedroom. "Be sure and close the window when you're through. It's cooled off at night and you mustn't get a chill."

"I'll remember."

Mary Margaret could protest all she wanted to, but I knew she would love to have a baby. And I knew she was happy for me, even though it looked like her marriage to Wesley was over. She hadn't heard from him in months.

I yawned, unplugged the iron and set it on the counter to cool. Six o'clock came early, and there always was a pile of dictation waiting on my desk for me to type. I couldn't imagine I'd ever thought the commander and the captain didn't need me.

The captain, bless his heart, could be pretty long-winded, and the chaplain showed his caring spirit by writing to families of the men who'd been killed or wounded. Unfortunately, it had become almost a full-time job for him, and I knew I only saw a fraction of the letters he actually wrote.

Both men were overly solicitous and careful to protect me from anything they thought might harm a woman "in your condition." Still, it always took me a good portion of every Friday to keep up with their work.

I started toward the bedroom, then remembered the window. *Better humor her,* I thought and walked back through the darkened living room. As I reached for the sash, the neighbor's dog began barking furiously. I thought I saw a shadow dart along the fence and then a glint of light. I blinked and it was gone. I studied the bushes for a dozen heartbeats, but nothing moved. The dog was quiet. I lowered the window, turned the latch and, just for good measure, pulled the shade.

* * *

Dotty cried when she found out I was expecting. "Oh, Celia, I'm so happy!" she blubbered into her handkerchief. "I'm going to be an aunt—well, not really"—she swished her hankie at Sam's raised eyebrows—"but I might as well be. Oh, I'm so excited I could scream."

"Please spare us that. And calm down, woman, before you scare the baby!" Sam grinned. "So when's the happy event?"

"The doctor says around the end of June."

"Well, let's have a toast." He raised his cup of hot cider. Dottie and I extended ours, and they touched in the air. "The three musketeers. Soon to be four—no, five counting Jake."

Dotty giggled.

"Hush, woman, you're breaking my concentration."

"Come on, you two, this cup is getting heavy!"

"All for one, and one for all. May we always be together."

Dotty never took her eyes off Sam. "Amen," she said and downed her cider in one gulp.

* * *

By Christmas Eve I still hadn't heard from Jake. The tree was up, and Aunt Rose had everybody busy stringing popcorn and making silver stars from candy bar and gum wrappers she'd been saving all year. The fruitcakes were sealed in colorful airtight cans with Norman Rockwell pictures on the lids. Most of us had decided to purchase war bonds with our Christmas money, but Uncle Edward saw to it that there was a gift for everyone under the tree, including one for Wesley and one for Jake. We'd mailed Billy's gift weeks ago, but of course we couldn't know when he'd receive it.

"Wesley can't have his until he writes," Mary Margaret had said stubbornly. But I thought it was worse to have it sitting right there under the tree.

"It will just remind her that he hasn't even called," I told Aunt Rose.

She shook her head. "That girl is stubborn, but she still loves him, Cissy. I think she wants to stay mad so she won't have to dwell on the fact that maybe he *can't* write or call."

"But wouldn't we have heard? I mean if he . . ."

Aunt Rose brushed a lock of graying hair out of her eyes and set the last plate on the table for Christmas day. "Only God knows, sweetheart. Only God knows for sure."

I stood back to admire Aunt Rose's handiwork. The table stretched out across the living room, both leaves in the middle and set with china and silver for eight. We were expecting three boys from the base for Christmas dinner and "who knows who else," Aunt Rose had said. "Maybe Jake will make it yet."

I tried to smile. "I don't think so. He would have called by now."

The truth was, although I'd have gladly given up anything to be with my husband, the sickness I'd lived with since October had increased and I felt worse than ever.

"Nerves," the captain had announced. "You need a glass of bitters. Perk you right up, and the baby too."

I had declined his invitation, as he'd declined ours to come for Christmas dinner.

"So good of you to ask, my dear," he'd said. "Please convey my apologies to your aunt. It seems my daughter has taken a notion to have me down to Arizona for the holiday. Beastly place. One should have snow and sleigh rides for Christmas, like the commander." Commander Drain had gone back to Minnesota for a week. "Ah, well . . . Have a good day. You deserve it. And I hope Jake makes it home in time to celebrate with you.

He's a good man, Celia. You can be proud of him."

"I am, sir. I really am." *I just wish this hateful war were over.*

"Oh dear, it's almost ten o'clock." Aunt Rose glanced at the clock. "The service starts at eleven, and we have one more choir practice. Mary Margaret," Aunt Rose called up the stairs, "are you ready? We leave in fifteen minutes. Celia, don't let your uncle forget the candles when you come. Mary Margaret and I are riding with the Hendersons."

The doorbell rang, and her head snapped toward the clock. "That must be them now. Of all times to be early!"

Chapter
Thirty-three

My goodness, Rose, relax. You'd think we'd never had a Christmas Eve before." But Uncle Edward smiled and touched her arm on his way to open the door.

"Praise God!"

Everyone froze at Uncle Edward's tone. Then the room erupted into shouts and tears and peals of joyful laughter.

"He's here, Celia," Aunt Rose gasped. "Oh, my stars, it's Wesley too. They made it home, the both of them."

Mary Margaret gripped my arm. "Wesley too! Celia what can I say to him? What will I do?"

"Tell him you love him," I whispered and ran into my husband's outstretched arms.

Both men looked wonderful, healthy and tan. Wesley had a shiner—"some slob took me for a sucker when I wasn't looking"—and a long jagged scar from his earlobe to the bottom of his chin.

Aunt Rose went to the candlelight service alone. She was home by midnight, bearing greetings and good wishes from everyone we knew.

The men told us how they'd met by chance in port at San Diego. They'd both managed to secure a four-day pass and decided to travel home together. "We wanted to surprise you," Jake said when I asked why they didn't call.

"We could have driven down and picked you up," Aunt Rose scolded.

"What? And have us miss the best ride of our lives?" Wesley seemed bent on entertaining us, and he refused to talk about his scars or the war.

"What ride?" Mary Margaret was eager to comply. I had a feeling she wanted to keep the conversation on neutral ground.

"We had to travel up Highway One a ways, and our first ride let us off at Oceanside. It was dark by then, but we got a ride from some br—woman in a pink Cadillac. I swear." He held up his right hand. "You tell them, Jake, they won't believe me."

"It's true," Jake chuckled, "every word of it, except you really had to be there to appreciate it."

"That's right," Wesley picked up the story again. "If you can imagine: It's dark, see, and this Cadillac convertible pulls up beside us, slows down to a crawl on the highway. No lights—we've still got blackout on the coast. Anyway, this dame with long blond hair done up in a scarf yells at us to hop in. So we throw our bags in back and jump into the moving car. Then she floors it. Just like that. Nearly threw old Jake here on his can. 'Slow down!' Jake yells from the back seat. I can't say nothing cause I'm picking bugs out of my teeth.

" 'Hang on,' she yodels like we aren't half deaf already from the wind. 'Don't you boys want some excitement in your lives?' Excitement. Can you beat that?

"So there we are, going a hundred miles an hour around these curves. Mountains on one side, cliffs and ocean on the other. No lights, no moon—it's dark as pitch out there. She suddenly throws on the brakes and makes a kamikaze right turn into the parking lot of this diner.

"She pulls up smooth as punch into a parking space and

invites us in for a Coke. 'On me, boys,' she says. 'Anything for our men in blue.'

"Turns out she's some actress from Hollywood, on her way to audition for a movie." Wesley took a sip of cocoa and wrinkled his nose. "She'd have brought us all the way, I bet. But Jake here wouldn't get back in the car." He shrugged and settled back on the sofa, like telling the story had used up all the steam he had left.

"Well, we made it anyway." Jake squeezed my hand.

"And just in time." Uncle Edward stood and stretched. "I don't know about all of you, but I'm beat. For once, I'm glad there are no little ones to get us up at the crack of dawn."

He looked at me and winked, but Jake missed it.

* * *

The sun was dancing through the window, glinting off the mirror on the dresser. Papa's picture fairly sparkled in its pewter frame, and I thought of Christmases long ago when we'd been up before the sun, Krista and I jumping up and down on Mama's side of the bed. "Hush now, both of you, and go fetch Chuckie," she would whisper.

Krista would stand quiet as a mouse trying not to wake the cat, while I lifted Chuckie from his crib and gave him a new diaper. Then we'd hurry into the bedroom and Mama would nuzzle Chuckie's ear, then put him on top of Papa.

"Da Da Da Da," Chuckie would croon and drool all over Papa's pajama top. But Papa never could get angry. He'd open one eye, snatch the baby and lift him high into the air. That was our cue to join them, and Krista and I would climb up on the bed and squeal, "It's Christmas, Papa, it's Christmas." "Can we check our stockings, Papa? Can we, please?"

Jake's "Good morning," and a hearty kiss, brought me back to the present.

I groaned and rolled onto his shoulder, loath to break the

magic of the night before. We'd been dreaming in a fairy tale called forever; I resented daylight and the reality it brought with it—even if it was Christmas.

My stomach churned. I jumped out of bed and dashed to the bathroom. When I could think again, I realized Jake still didn't know.

I found him sitting on the edge of Mary Margaret's old bed struggling into the pants he'd kicked off the night before. He looked up in concern when I eased back into the room and shut the door. "What's wrong, babe? Are you sick? Of course you are. But . . ."

"Shh." I put my finger to my lips and sat gingerly beside him on the bed. "No one else is up."

I fought down another bout of nausea and took his hand. "This is all your fault, you know," I said and placed it on my quivering stomach. I watched his puzzled frown turn to wonder, then a smile of delight.

"You're not! I mean, are we—?"

I nodded. "The last part of June or early July."

Then I was on my way back to the bathroom.

* * *

It was hours later before I had the chance to ask about Wesley. "I can't believe he came," I said when we were once again in the privacy of our own room.

"Let's just say I persuaded him."

"Jake!"

Now I knew how Wesley had really gotten that black eye.

"But he outranks you. What if—?"

He shrugged. "It's a family matter, babe, nothing to do with rank and he knows it. I'm not sure it did much good though. He still swears their marriage was a mistake, and he's probably right. But at least now they can discuss it face to face."

"How long?"

"We have to report for duty by 0700 Monday morning. That's two more days. We'll drop Mary Margaret and Wesley at your place tomorrow morning, then spend some time with my folks. Pa said he'd run Wesley and me back to San Diego in the truck."

He laid his tie across the dresser and shucked the uniform blouse over his head. When he was comfortable in just a skivvy shirt and trousers, he propped himself on my bed, his back to the wall, and patted the spot next to him.

I crawled up and tried to snuggle into his shoulder, but he turned sideways so he could look into my eyes.

"Detective Harman called, Celia. Right after I talked to my folks. He said to tell you they'd arrested a man in connection with another assault. He needs you to come down and tell your story again. Something about what happened in the alley? Seems there are some things my wife neglected to tell me."

He kept his fingers under my chin and his eyes fixed on my face. I had no idea what he saw there. If I'd had one of Mama's quilts handy, I'd have crawled under it, like Chuckie when Mama had to dose him with castor oil.

"Jake, I'm sorry. I just didn't want to worry you. You were so far away, and there was nothing you could do about it."

"What happened, Celia?" he said quietly.

I told the whole thing, from Hyatt's sudden interest in our office to his following me around and showing up at our apartment. When I got to the part about the alley, I could see the muscles in Jake's face twitch, but he sat perfectly still.

"My neck was sore for a while, but the worst part was they didn't believe me." Telling it made me angry all over again. "He was trying to choke me, Jake, but I don't know why. The police thought . . ."

"What were *you* thinking, Celia?"

"What?"

"Why did you go into that alley? You knew you might be in danger, or did you forget about the thugs who tried to kill you before?"

I couldn't believe I was hearing this.

"Jake Freeman, are you suggesting it was my fault?"

His eyes were focused on the ceiling where a moth, trapped in the light fixture, fluttered and flopped, trying to escape.

"Does he smoke?"

"Who?"

"This Hyatt character. Do you know if he smokes?"

I tried to picture him in the hallway, by the elevator, talking to Mrs. Dillon. "I don't know. I don't remember seeing him with a cigarette. The other one does though. The one in the alley . . . when I was close to him . . . his shirt . . ." I let my voice trail off. Sergeant Harman had asked about cigarettes too. "Jake, you can't think Mr. Hyatt was involved in the attack on Sam and me?"

He didn't answer.

"Darling, that's ridiculous. It certainly wasn't Mr. Hyatt who tried to choke me. He's a politician, for goodness sake. Why would he risk his reputation?"

Jake drew a deep breath and let it out slowly. I knew he was trying to stay in control. He'd never used his temper on me, but he was a scrapper as a kid and I saw what he had done to Wesley's eye.

He shifted his gaze back to my face. "Don't," he swallowed, then continued as if he'd read my mind, "don't ever keep anything like that from me again. You're my wife, Celia. If that guy . . ." His hands were shaking as he pulled me into his arms and buried his face in my hair. I could barely hear his muffled words.

"If he'd have hurt you, God help me, I swear I'd kill him."

Chapter
Thirty-four

Ma Freeman had boiled the turkey bones from Christmas dinner for a hearty soup.

"I growed the taters and onions on my own," ten-year-old John boasted around a mouthful of his mother's buttermilk biscuits.

"Did not!" his eight-year-old brother protested. "I helped. Tell them, Ma."

"You two hush. Jake and Celia didn't come here to listen to a bunch of squabbling younguns."

Jake's pa helped himself to a fifth biscuit. "Pass the margarine and some of that peach jam. I swear, old woman, you did yourself proud today."

Mrs. Freeman's face was flushed from the heat of the kitchen and trying to keep her brood in check, but she fairly glowed with her husband's compliment.

Why, she's really beautiful when she smiles. I vowed to try and make it happen more often.

Anne Marie helped her mother and me clear the table, then donned an apron to start the dishes.

"Leave those be for now." Her mother put the last of the soup in the icebox by the stove and held the kitchen door for both of us. "We have some visiting to do. It's not often I have all my children together anymore."

She held her head high, chin stuck slightly forward as if daring either of us to mention Tim.

Anne Marie told me later that her mother refused to talk about her second son—his life or his death. "It's like Tim was never born," she sighed. "She won't talk about me going either, but I have to, Celia," she said desperately, like she needed my approval. "I'm a nurse, and they need nurses. You understand, don't you?"

I held her hand. "Yes, Anne. Yes, I do. But it's easy to see how your mama might not."

Of the girls, Anne looked the most like Jake. She didn't have his crooked nose or thick dark brows, but she had his eyes— huge brown jewels sparkling in a tiny face—with a bow-shaped mouth and slightly pointed chin. She looked fragile, like Snow White in the fairy tale. But her chin had a lift to it, and there was a spark of determination in her eyes.

"I can't stay here forever," she said. "Mama has Sarah June and the boys to help. Besides, they'll be better off with one less mouth to feed. But will you help me, Celia? Stay here while I tell Ma? I leave the day after tomorrow, and I haven't had the nerve to say a thing."

What could I do? I nodded and went with her into the sitting room. Jake and his father were talking baseball while his mother sat contentedly on one end of the sofa, darning a pair of little boy's socks.

No one said anything for two minutes after Anne's announcement. Then Mr. Freeman shrugged. "You do what you got to do, girl," he said hoarsely. "We won't stand in your way." He looked pointedly at Ma Freeman, who was staring straight ahead, the same determined tilt to her chin, like she hadn't heard a word Anne said.

* * *

Jake and I left early and walked the five blocks to our hotel room. "It's just one night," Jake had said to justify the expense. "Wesley and Mary Margaret need their privacy, and so do we." He slipped an arm around my shoulders. "Anyway, we have an appointment downtown at six o'clock."

I looked at him curiously. "What appointment?"

Jake shut the door to the dingy room and turned on the light. "With Sergeant Harman."

I felt like someone had punched me in the stomach. "Jake, no! Why now? We have so little time together. Can't it wait?"

"I want some answers, Celia."

"Answers to what?" I tried to collect my thoughts. I'd told Sergeant Harman I couldn't identify the man who'd assaulted me. The alley had been in shadow, and the man was dressed in black. I never even saw his face.

My stomach churned. "Do you really think this attack on me might have something to do with us?"

"That's what I'm trying to find out."

The bus ride to town took twenty minutes, and I felt like I was sharing it with a stranger.

Jake kept quiet while I told the whole thing again and Sergeant Harman took notes in his little black book. When we were through, he tried to usher us out of the office, but Jake wouldn't budge.

Harman wasn't very cooperative. He listened to Jake's questions and talked all around them—*like a politician*, I thought. Jake finally stood, every muscle in his body taut, and leaned against the desk, his clenched fists pressing into the wood.

"Listen, Harman. My wife has been molested. Her father was executed, and a good friend is crippled for life because these creeps don't want witnesses to a murder. More than one, I'd guess. And now I want to know two things. I want to know who tried to kill my wife, and I want to know what I have to do to protect my family while I'm gone. Because I swear to you, sergeant, I will protect them—one way or another."

I realized he was talking as if our baby were already born. I couldn't help but feel a surge of pride and love for the man I'd married.

Harman smiled and waved Jake back to his seat. "Okay, kid, sit down." He pressed his hands together in a pyramid and rested his chin against them as if deep in thought. When he looked up, he was looking at me. "The truth is, we are working on some evidence that could link Roy Cummings with your father and a money-laundering operation. My guess is, whoever killed Cummings took part in the Berdowski murder and the scheme to pin it on your father. When we catch up with him . . . Well, let's just say the mob is pretty protective of their own unless one of them's in danger of being skinned," he chuckled. "Then they tend to squeal like a stuck pig."

He stood, and I knew the interview was over. "Your wife will be safe, Mr. Freeman, I can guarantee that. It's only a matter of time before we have this all wrapped up. So," he warned as he ushered us out the door, "don't do anything stupid. You might jeopardize the case. If these goons walk, your wife's life won't be worth a plug nickel. Got it?"

Jake dipped his chin in a curt nod.

"Have a good evening, Mrs. Freeman." The detective smiled somewhere over my shoulder. "We'll keep you posted."

I'm sure you will, I thought sarcastically as Jake led me down two flights of stairs and out onto the cool air.

* * *

I didn't want Jake to go, but both of us knew we had no choice.

"It won't be long, babe, I promise. This war can't last forever. Besides," he rested his hand gently over my navel, "I have two people to come home to now."

Wesley was waiting outside when Jake's pa pulled into the driveway. Jake and I had already said our good-bys. I didn't want to cry in front of Mr. Freeman. Anyway, tears would only make Jake feel worse, so I took the hand Wesley held out to help me down and let him take my place in the truck. He had a hard look on his face, stubborn and defiant. His scar quivered when I said, "Good-by, Wesley, take care," and he wouldn't meet Jake's eyes at all.

I watched the truck disappear around the corner and pulled my coat higher against the chill. Raindrops big as snowflakes began to dot the sidewalk. "Elephant tears," Mama used to call them.

"Are there elephants in heaven, Mama?" Krista had asked.

"Don't be silly," I had blurted before Mama could answer her. "And anyway, elephants don't cry."

Krista frowned and clutched Mama's leg. "Do they cry, Mama? Do they?"

Mama had bent and kissed her hair. "Hush now, child. Of course they do. At one time or another, all God's creatures cry."

I remember feeling foolish and ashamed.

* * *

Mary Margaret wouldn't talk about her time alone with Wesley. "I don't think there's much chance, Celia. It would take all God's power to change Wesley and make our marriage work. And why should God be bothered with the likes of me?"

"Because he loves you, that's why."

But she wasn't listening.

It rained off and on the entire month of January. On the twelfth, Jake called to say their training mission was over and they were leaving San Diego soon. He couldn't say for where, of course, and my heart ached with the thought of another long separation.

Please, God, keep him safe. It was a prayer I was to whisper a million times in the months to come.

I prayed a lot for Mary Margaret too. She pretended to be gay, dancing with the soldiers at the USO or going to parties every Saturday night. But more times than not I'd hear her cry herself to sleep. One day I knocked on her door and tried to comfort her, but she yelled at me to go away.

"I don't need you. I don't need anybody. Just go!"

She had dinner waiting when I got home that evening. "I'm sorry, Celia. I don't know what gets into me."

She apologized, but I didn't try to pry again.

Chapter
Thirty-five

I looked forward to Saturdays at the USO—and even more to church on Sundays, where I shared one end of a hard-backed pew with Dotty and Sam. We sat in the same one every Sunday, right up front where Sam could wheel his chair through the side door and park it on the end.

Sam had become more and more resourceful. He seemed to have come to grips with his limitations, physically anyway. He'd learned he could do almost anything from his chair and had become more confident and self-assured.

"Maybe *too* self-assured," Dotty confided one Saturday evening at the USO. "What if he finds he doesn't need me at all?"

"Don't be a goose," I said, adding the last can of fruit juice to the punch, and opened the double window to the serving bar. "Sam needs you for other reasons, and you know it."

Soldiers, sailors and marines were milling in the cavernous room. Some of the girls, dressed in short skirts and tight blouses, moved in and out among the crowd serving sandwiches and accepting invitations to dance.

Mary Margaret stood over in the corner talking with the volunteer who operated our new record player. The woman smiled, then nodded, and Mary Margaret moved away to join a marine lieutenant at his table. She took his hand, laughing and batting the false eyelashes she'd bought at Woolworth's the day before.

The needle scratched, then Rudy Vallee began to croon "As Time Goes By," and couples stood to dance. Mary Margaret pulled the lieutenant to his feet, and soon they were floating around the room, her head on his shoulder, his arm planted firmly around her waist.

"It'll work out, girl." I felt Dotty's hand on my shoulder and knew she was watching them too. "That cousin of yours has a hard head, but one of these days God will get through to her."

"Dotty, look." I nodded toward a group that had just entered the hall. The last person held the door for a man in a wheelchair.

"Sam!" She untied her apron and threw it on the counter. "He never comes here. What if something's wrong?"

She grabbed my arm and dragged me past the warming oven and refrigerator to the kitchen door. Sam was already there.

"Well, if it's not the two prettiest girls in the universe." Sam's smile looked forced and his face was pale. I suddenly felt afraid.

"Sam," Dotty sounded breathless. "What is it?"

He winced and looked at me. "Can you take over for her, Celia? I need Dot to drive me to the hospital."

Dotty grabbed hold of the door frame, and I thought she was going to faint.

"What's wrong?" I asked.

"My leg. The right one. The pain is getting worse by the minute."

"But, Sam, you can't feel your legs. How . . . ?"

"*Couldn't* feel my legs. The right one hurts like crazy now. The doc wants to see me right away."

He turned to Dotty, who stood dumbfounded in the doorway. "Will you put some gas in it, girl? This isn't getting any better."

I didn't even think that Sam might want Dotty to himself.

I just grabbed our bags, yelled at Mary Margaret to watch the kitchen and headed out the door behind them.

The doctor didn't offer much hope. "I still don't think there's much chance you'll walk again. There has been some response in the nerve endings, though. Not much we can do about it now. Let's wait and see how it progresses. I'll give you something to help with the pain."

Neither Dotty nor I knew what to say. Sam had been through so much and come out all the stronger for it. What was happening to him now?

* * *

Jake had made it clear he wanted me to leave Wildish and Hyatt. "Until we know for sure that Hyatt isn't part of this, I want you away from there, you hear?"

It had been on the tip of my tongue to remind him it was Hyatt who'd been shadowing me, but I didn't like to cause a fuss. It was getting harder to sit at a desk all day anyway, and both Mr. Wildish and Mr. Hyatt said they understood when I turned in my thirty-day notice.

I had just sent off a letter telling Jake I'd be staying home as of April 1, when Aunt Rose called to read me a letter from Billy.

March 15, 1944

Dear Mom and Dad,

Thank you for the fruitcake. Surprised ya, huh? Well, you can't be as surprised as I was when I looked up from cleaning my rifle and saw Jake standing in front of me, grinning like an idiot. He didn't care that there were at least a hundred men standing around, he grabbed me and held me for what seemed like an hour. Boy, I've never had a better hug.

We didn't have much time to talk, he had to get back to the ship, but he told me to stand by, he had a present for me from home. He sent the fruitcake back in the launch. Of course, all the guys had to have a bite, and by the time it got to me there were only crumbs. But just knowing you baked it, Mom, made them the best crumbs I've ever tasted.

Wow, what a day. I'll dream about this for the rest of the war.

I love you all, Billy

P.S. Jake said Cissy is going to have a baby. That's great news. Tell her to take good care of my future second cousin.

I hadn't been off the phone ten minutes when the postman brought a letter Jake had written the same day.

March 15, 1944

Dear Celia,

Well, we're off again tomorrow, after twenty days at anchor (you know I can't say where). I haven't had a chance to write till now, but two things happened I have to tell you.

I finally got my promotion! All that work paid off and your husband is now a Petty Officer 1st Class. How about that? To celebrate I took a work crew ashore, where we unloaded supplies and handed out rations to some troops that have been there awhile. They were sure glad to see us—we had oranges and they hadn't had fresh fruit in months.

Anyway, I was shooting the breeze with some of them, when I looked across the compound and saw a young GI sitting on a stump polishing his rifle. We started kidding around about how crazy it was to keep your weapon shined when just one patrol would get it filthy again. Something about him looked familiar so I asked, and one of the men said, "Aw, that's just Billy-boy. He's a preacher's kid or something from southern California."

Well, I knew right then he wasn't any preacher's kid, but our own Billy in the flesh! We were both so excited. Tell Aunt Rose I hugged him hard enough for all of us. Also be sure and tell her that he's fine and I gave him the fruitcake she sent with me.

Between you and me, babe, he's skinny as a rail and has a rash from head to toe, but he's no worse off than any of the others. He'll be right as rain in no time when this thing ends.

I gotta go. Tell my little one I love her. Yes, I hope it's a girl—a man couldn't have it better than to have another angel like you. I love you, babe.

Forever yours, Jake

"I miss Jake so much," I told Dotty that night. "And Billy too. I hope and pray they'll both be home soon."

Chapter
Thirty-six

Mama would say I didn't have the sense God gave a goose, which is precious little if you stop to think about it. And I hardly gave it a second thought when Mr. Wildish asked me to work late one Tuesday night in March.

"Go on ahead, Dotty," I insisted when she hesitated. "I'll grab a sandwich at Woolworth's and have this brief done up in no time."

Woolworth's was crowded. I gobbled down a hot dog and a glass of milk, but it was almost six-thirty before I got back to the office. The brief took longer than I expected. I looked up at seven to see Mr. Wildish standing at my desk and Miss Kraus waiting by the door.

"I'm leaving now, Mrs. Freeman. Mr. Hyatt is in his office down the hall. Working on his acceptance speech, no doubt. I trust you'll be finished soon?"

I nodded. "Yes, sir. I should only be a few more minutes."

If I felt any misgivings about being alone in the building with Mr. Hyatt, they were relieved when Elmer, the building super, poked his head through the door.

"I'm on duty tonight, Miss Celia. If there's anything you need, you holler, hear?"

An hour later, I stacked the neatly typed pages on Mr. Wildish's desk. *Eight-thirty! Where did the time go?* I gathered my things and rang for the elevator. When the doors opened, there was Mr. Hyatt talking to Elmer. Hyatt's tie was loose, and he had rolled up his shirtsleeves.

"Miss Celia"—Elmer tipped his hat—"I'm afraid the next bus won't be here for a while. You can sure wait in my cubby if you like."

"There's no need for that." Mr. Hyatt motioned me into the elevator. "I'll ride back down with you, and my driver will take you home."

"Mr. Hyatt, I couldn't, I . . ."

He looked annoyed. "Don't be foolish, Celia. It's late. We wouldn't want people to accuse us of overworking you." He looked pointedly at my growing belly, and I felt myself flush.

"You best listen, Miss Celia." Elmer spoke up. "You do look some peaked to me."

I realized Elmer was right. I was tired and hungry. *Maybe Mary Margaret left some dinner in the fridge.*

Mr. Hyatt made a phone call, and within five minutes the Rolls pulled up to the curb. The driver didn't even turn his head as Hyatt ushered me into the back seat and gave him directions.

The driver was not much inclined to conversation, and after a few inquiries with only "Yes, ma'am" and "No, ma'am" for replies, I closed my eyes and thought about Jake.

I must have fallen asleep. When I opened my eyes I realized the car had stopped and the driver was opening the door. But instead of letting me out, he forced his way onto the seat. At the same instant, I realized we were nowhere near my apartment.

He grabbed me, and I swung out with my fist, grazing his forehead and knocking off his hat. His eyes glittered like tiny fluorescent beads I saw once in a Halloween display: bat's eyes, predatory and malicious.

I gasped as he forced my arms behind my back and bound them with a narrow rope. I screamed once, but his slap took my breath away and I thought about the danger to my child. He tied a rag around my eyes and pushed me to the floor.

"Stay there," he hissed, "and don't move, or I'll kill you now and be done with it."

The odor on his breath and clothing was so foul I turned my face into the carpeted floorboards. *That awful smell!* It was nauseating, but familiar. Suddenly I realized this was the same man who had tried to choke me. But this time there was no Miss Kraus to come to my rescue.

God, help me! It was a silent cry, and I prayed like I'd never prayed before.

I heard the motor turn and felt the car glide onto the roadway. I had no idea where we were. I only knew I was a long way from the city. *And a long way from help.*

What I couldn't understand was why. I'd never seen this man before, except for that day in the alley. Or had I? Could he have been involved in the attack on Sam and me? And did it all have something to do with my father? Why would someone want me dead?

It was all too much. I quit my mental wrestling and tried to concentrate on where we were going, but the car drove straight ahead, no stops or turns to memorize.

After what seemed like hours we turned left onto a gravel road, traveled what felt like a few yards and stopped.

The driver opened the door and jerked me upright from my cramped position. My legs refused to hold me at first, and he gripped my shoulders until I could stand on my own.

I heard a coyote call, then silence, broken only by a splashing sound. The whistling wind brought a heavy scent of pine to the chill night air, and suddenly I knew where we were.

"Move!" He punctuated his command with a hard shove. Only his unrelenting grip on my arm kept me from falling.

We had moved ahead only a few steps, when he cursed and pulled me to a stop. "I'm gonna take the blinder off. I can't drag you all the way."

He untied the rag, and for a minute everything stayed black. Gradually, light from a quarter-moon revealed my surroundings.

Bear Lake.

I felt the baby move inside me and knew that, if I didn't act, my child would never see the moon, or smell the wind, or hear the water lap against the shore.

I plunged ahead. *God, please show me what to do.* No sooner had I whispered my prayer than we reached the spot where the rocks made a jagged trail down to the beach. I felt the driver hesitate, then watched as he looked around for the easiest way down.

He doesn't know the area! I bit my lip to keep from crying out with joy. *If he's unfamiliar with this place, maybe I can break away.* A picture of the rickety old boathouse flashed through my mind, and I knew what I had to do.

I let him lead me halfway down. My hands were still tied, but my legs had recovered their strength, though I was careful not to let him see that. We had reached the trickiest spot, where two boulders formed a crevice with a sheer ten-foot drop to more rocks below.

I knew there was no way out of there. The last time Jake and I had come, some boys dropped their keys into the pit. Two of them lowered the third one down. He found the keys all right, but it had taken four policemen and a special sling to get him out.

I waited until my body was pointed in the right direction, then pretended to stumble. As I staggered forward, I pulled my captor off balance. Just as I had hoped, he released the grip on my arm to keep from falling himself. I spun around quickly, kicked out with my left foot and jammed my elbow into his side. With a series of oaths that would have made even Captain Long blush, he plunged sideways into the ravine.

I didn't wait around to see how he was, but stepped carefully on a narrow flat-top rock to the right of the boulder, then onto the trail that led to the beach below. Once I hit the sand I ran like the devil was chasing me—like Joe DiMaggio going for a double. I kept the pace until I rounded the familiar curve of rock and almost collided with the side of the boathouse.

I leaned against the rotting boards. By the time I caught my breath, I realized the cold wind, blowing off the water, had penetrated my flimsy sweater. My teeth were chattering, and I knew I had to take shelter.

I tried to pry the boards off the front door to the shack, but they wouldn't budge. I thought I heard voices and a scraping sound, but when I turned there was no one. I ran around the shack until I finally found three loose boards and squeezed inside.

The shack looked like a scrap yard, with pieces of wood and rusted steel flung helter-skelter across the floor. I heard a rustling in the corner and flung a hand across my mouth to keep from crying out. But it was only a disgruntled coon, upset by having its nap disturbed.

One rowboat was still intact. I grabbed a piece of tarp from a peg on the wall and crawled into the bottom of the boat. Reason told me that even if the driver had survived the fall uninjured, he could not possibly climb out of his rock prison. But I couldn't stop shaking. I jumped at every sound.

I tried not to think about the long night ahead. It would be hours before anyone realized I was missing. Mary Margaret wouldn't get home from work until after nine tomorrow morning. Even then she might think I'd just stayed with Dot.

My thoughts spun. Every time I closed my eyes, I saw Roy Cummings's face. Roy at the carnival, hiding behind a tree, talking with that other man in the alley next to Key Hole Nelson's Bar.

Roy flashing a grotesque smile from the bottom of a pickle barrel—"I fooled you, girl. Your father may be dead, but I'm not." Another man, in a dark coat and glossy black boots, peered into the barrel. His eyes gleamed as he picked up a hammer and began to nail down the lid, his laughter drowning out Roy's screams.

I must have slept. When the baby's furious kicking woke me, light had begun to filter through the cracks in the boards. I heard a hawk cry as it dove for its breakfast, and I realized I was famished.

It took me several minutes to get the blood circulating to my hands and feet. I made my way cautiously back up the beach, watching and listening for anything out of place.

The lake was deserted. There were still patches of snow here and there among the upper rocks, and I marveled at how I had been protected last night. My body felt bruised, like I'd been put through a wringer, and I smelled like I'd slept with the coon. But I was alive.

When I reached the bend where the trail connected with the rocks, I stopped to listen, but there was no sound from below. I hurried on without looking down.

As I neared the top of the cliff, I could see the smooth, rounded fender of the Rolls, and three steps farther brought me face to face with the policeman who was carefully examining it.

Chapter
Thirty-seven

Mr. Hyatt's driver turned out to be a man named Malcomb "Shrimp" Stiles, a hit man for hire by anyone who wanted a dirty job done.

"It's the same creep who ran us down that night," Sam insisted. But Detective Harman refused to give us any information "that might jeopardize the case."

Mr. Hyatt denied any knowledge of the "Shrimp's" background. But everyone took notice when he suddenly had to go "out of town on campaign business" two days after Stiles's arrest.

The police had questioned him, of course, but let him go for lack of evidence. "Be patient, Mr. Crandall," he told Uncle Edward. "We can't arrest a man like Hyatt without hard evidence. He'd turn the tables and have us all in court. Ha ha."

"I didn't know Sergeant Harman had a sense of humor," I whispered as he and his partner climbed back into their car.

"I didn't notice." Sam rubbed his hands up and down his legs. I knew they ached terribly, but it was also a gesture he repeated whenever he was aggravated. He wanted an end to this thing. We all did.

The rest of March and April seemed to fly. I never went back to Wildish and Hyatt except to clean out my desk. The doctor had pronounced the baby and me healthy in spite of our ordeal, but suggested I "stay home and take it easy." I was determined to follow his advice. Besides, even though Jake was somewhere in the South Pacific, blissfully ignorant of the situation, I knew he would have it no other way.

* * *

"Celia Freeman, I can't believe you're doing this. You're big as a house, and besides it's only May!"

I ignored Mary Margaret's scolding and finished packing my towel, a book and a stack of tuna sandwiches into a wicker basket I'd borrowed from Captain Long. "By all means, keep it, my dear," he'd said when I asked if I could use it. "I've no use for the thing. It just gets in the way." I threw in two apples for good measure and turned to my exasperating cousin. "I'm going to the beach." I said emphatically. "Are you coming or not?"

She looked in the mirror and rubbed her face as if to smooth away some imaginary lines. "Oh, all right. I can't let you go alone. But you have to promise we'll come home if I start to get red. I refuse to live through another burn."

We had just stepped outside to the porch when a late-model Ford pulled in the drive and Uncle Edward stepped out of the passenger side. I looked closer and saw the driver was Sergeant Harman.

What now? I couldn't help the stab of anxiety I felt when I saw the sergeant. The only time he came around was in response to trouble.

But Uncle Edward had a smile on his face, and if I didn't know better, I'd have said Sergeant Harman looked happy too. Well, not exactly happy, but pleased with himself.

I set the basket on the step and moved down the walk to greet Uncle Edward. My gait was awkward on the uneven ground, and he reached past my growing belly to steady me.

"Come back inside, sweetheart, we have some great news."

He hugged Mary Margaret, then led us into the apartment with the sergeant following behind. I offered lemonade, but no one was interested.

"It's over, Celia," Uncle Edward said as soon as we were seated. "Everyone involved in Lou Berdowski's murder has been arrested. They go to trial in a week. Tell her, sergeant."

Sergeant Harman looked uncomfortable. He perched on the edge of a straightback chair and loosened his tie. "We finally caught up with Robert Hyatt. That slime Stiles sang like a canary when we offered him a deal. Spilled the whole thing from start to finish: your father's part in the bank theft, the Berdowski murder, the frame-up. He gave up four big shots, including Hyatt, in exchange for his own neck."

My hands felt cold, and my mouth was dry as sand. "How was Mr. Hyatt involved?"

"Hyatt was peanuts back when your father was arrested. He was involved with your father and Lou Berdowski in the money scheme. He hired Roy Cummings to frame your father, but someone higher up had ordered it.

"Hyatt must have been feeling pretty safe with Berdowski dead and your father out of the way. His pockets were loaded with nice clean cash, and he had the backing of a pretty powerful cartel."

The sergeant settled back against the chair and actually smiled, enjoying his tale. My mind burned with a thousand questions, but I decided to let him finish.

"Hyatt was actually a pawn. Someone saw to it that he skirted by the law exams and landed a partnership with Wildish, a friend of Hyatt's uncle. The rest is history. They must have needed another politician in their pocket. No doubt he'd have won the race for Congress," Harman smiled directly at me, "except you came along and made him nervous."

I looked at Uncle Edward. He shook his head, so I kept quiet and let the sergeant finish.

Harman nodded as if I'd spoken. "Hyatt was with Roy Cummings that day in the alley when you and Jake overheard their scheme. He'd already had one run-in with Jake when he stumbled into his fight with Roy. Hyatt had no idea how much you knew, or if you could identify him. But with his political career at stake, he couldn't take a chance. He needed you out of the way, so he hired the same thug who had tried to kill you before."

"Stiles was the one who—?"

"Right. When we reopened the case after Cummings was murdered, someone decided you and Jake were dangerous and ordered a hit. Only the 'Shrimp' loused it up and got Sam instead.

"When you went to work for Wildish and Hyatt, you were like a pig on a platter." Harman's face turned red. "Excuse my expression. But Hyatt saw it as an opportunity to put you out of his life for good.

"The 'Shrimp's' neck was in the noose after that botched hit and run, so he was eager to please when Hyatt asked him to pose as his driver and wait for the 'right opportunity' to do you in."

I looked down at my hands and realized they were shaking. "Who . . . ?" I wanted to ask who had killed Lou Berdowski, but I couldn't get it out.

Uncle Edward must have known. He put his arm around me and held me as close as he could. "It doesn't matter, sweetheart. They got him. That's all you need to know."

Harman nodded. "They all have files thick enough to put them away for a hundred years."

He stood, snatched his hat from the table and turned to the

door. "Tell your husband you're safe now, Mrs. Freeman. And your father's name is cleared." He looked at Uncle Edward, then back at me. "I'm sorry. I know it won't bring him back. I hope this helps."

I buried my face in Uncle Edward's shoulder. I felt fourteen again, miserable, scared and angry with God. "All these years," I sobbed. "All the prayers that we would find the real murderers and clear Papa's name. Now my prayer has been answered and it doesn't help. It doesn't help at all."

"It's a beginning," Uncle Edward said quietly. "The burden's been lifted, now you can let it go."

I took the handkerchief he offered and blew my nose.

"Thank God," Mary Margaret sighed when Uncle Edward and the detective were gone. "Maybe now life will get back to normal."

"Us?" I laughed. "With a family like ours, our lives will never be normal."

We all thought it was a joke.

Chapter
Thirty-eight

After the telegram. After the initial tears. After the flowers and the flag. After the three rounds of seven jarred our rigid bodies and the last shaking-sad note of "Taps" echoed across the spring-green hills, we got a letter from a man named Wallace Heart.

Dear Mr. and Mrs. Crandall,

Your son Billy was a friend of mine and I just thought you should know he died a hero.

We were on routine patrol when a barrage of fire came at us out of nowhere. We hit the ground rolling and landed in a ravine behind a clump of _____. It was good cover, but the shooting stopped and we couldn't see the enemy.

Billy-boy and I had blood all over us, but neither of us had been hit. Then we heard Sarge scream and saw him out there in the open, bleeding like a son-of-a-gun. He'd got it in both legs and couldn't move—just kept screaming at us to kill him, kill him before they got to him, you know?

Before I could stop him, Billy ran out, grabbed him under the arms and started dragging him back toward the ditch. They almost made it. If it's any consolation, he didn't feel any pain.

The snipers were a couple of kids, stranded when their outfit left the island. They surrendered when another patrol came along to rescue us. I think they were glad to give it up, just to get some food.

I'm sorry about Billy. He was a good kid. I miss him.

Yours Truly, PFC Wallace Heart

* * *

Uncle Edward wore the pain of Billy's death like a dagger in his heart. He sat stiff and quiet through the funeral, a rock for the rest of us to lean on, but bleeding to death inside.

Mary Margaret went to pieces. Aunt Rose turned from one chore to another, seeing to everyone else's comfort, escaping to her room when she felt the need for tears.

I felt numb. Billy. The little boy who had made me feel welcomed my first day with the family. The ten-year-old who'd taught me to catch and throw. The pesky adolescent who'd replaced Chuckie as my brother. Now he was gone too, and I couldn't take it in.

The baby seemed to sense my need for peace. Instead of the flailing, jabbing movements of arms and legs against my rib cage, she shifted to a gentle rolling with long periods of quiet in between.

"Nothing to worry about, Mrs. Freeman," the doctor told me as he put away his stethoscope and helped me slide off the table. "The baby's fine. It's settling into position. A few more weeks and this will all be over."

He handed me my bag from the chair by the door. "Call me if you have any pain. Oh, and I'm sorry about your brother."

I didn't bother to correct him.

* * *

Sam and Dotty got engaged in June right after school was out. Sam had graduated with honors, a feat that got him scholarship money for the university law school.

Dotty said she was almost afraid to tell me about the engagement, with Billy's funeral only three weeks past and the baby due anytime. But there was no way they could keep it secret. It was written all over both their faces. They glowed with happiness, and Dotty actually bounced when she walked. Then, of course, there was the ring. I oohed and ahed over the star-cut diamonds, three of them in a solid-gold setting.

"Wow, Mr. and Mrs. Warbucks." I hugged them both and kissed Sam on the cheek. "I'm so happy for you! When?"

"We're not sure yet." Dotty looked shyly down at Sam, who reached up and captured the hand she had rested on his shoulder. "That's the other news. Tell her, Sam."

He brought her hand to his lips and kissed it. "You go ahead, love, you're doing fine."

"They're going to do surgery on his legs, Celia. The right one anyway, and maybe, later on, the left. The doctors think it's possible he'll walk again. If the left one responds, that is."

"How's the pain?" I asked Sam, who shrugged and rubbed his palm against his right thigh.

"It's under control."

Dotty rolled her eyes. "Sure—when he takes his medication, which isn't near often enough."

Sam raised his eyebrows at her in a perfect Groucho Marx imitation. Neither of us could help but laugh.

"Like I said, it's under control. Besides," he was serious now, "I'd rather feel the pain than nothing. If the Lord wants to heal me, I'll put up with whatever it takes."

We were still standing in the doorway to Sam's apartment. He backed his chair farther into the cluttered room and waved me toward a clear spot on the sofa.

Dotty handed us each a glass of lemonade and moved a pile of books off the only other chair in the room. "I can't wait to get my hands on this apartment."

Sam picked up a discarded sofa pillow and threw it in her direction.

"All right, you two, you never answered my question. When's the wedding, or haven't you set a date?"

"That's just it." Dotty set her glass down on the table. "We can't set a date until we know the outcome of the surgery. It's scheduled for August. Sam needs to get back to classes in October, so we're thinking sometime in the early fall."

"Or Christmas, if this thing with my leg takes longer than expected."

Christmas. What would it be like this year? We'd have the baby, of course, but there would be empty places at the table that no one on earth could fill. Would Jake be home, or Wesley? I couldn't bear to think that far ahead.

The baby kicked, snapping me out of my reverie.

"Are you okay?" Dotty and Sam were watching me, expressions of concern on their faces.

"I'm fine." I stood to give my little passenger more room. "The doctor said these last few weeks would be difficult. I just wish I could get comfortable for five minutes."

*　*　*

Jake phoned on June 29.

"Can you hear me, babe? The static on this end is terrible." He didn't wait for my answer. "I got worried when I didn't hear. Are you all right? The baby . . ."

"We're fine, Jake, but your daughter is stubborn. She refuses to come out into this cold cruel world."

"Takes after her old man already, huh?"

There was a long pause. Had we been cut off? The thought made me panic, like there was so much left unsaid. It was bad enough he couldn't be here when our baby was born. I couldn't help but wonder if I'd ever hear his voice again.

"Celia?"

Chapter Thirty-eight

"I'm here, darling."

"I love you. You know that."

"I love you too, Jake. Please come home soon."

"Have your uncle send a wire as soon as it's over, okay?"

"He knows that. We've rehearsed it a hundred times; Aunt Rose will call our friends and Uncle Edward will send the telegram." I paused. "Jake?"

This time the line was really dead.

Epilogue

I wiped out the lid to the cake saver Dotty had given me last Christmas and covered the remains of Libby's birthday cake. Libby had already licked the candles clean and retired to the living room to watch *The Donna Reed Show*.

The others had left over an hour ago. Aunt Rose and Uncle Edward had a two-hour drive and had promised to drop Mary Margaret on the way. Tomorrow was Sunday, and Dot wanted to get her brood home by bedtime. Her youngest, John, could be a holy terror if he didn't get his sleep; she didn't want another summons during the morning service to rescue him from the church nursery—or, rather, the church nursery from him.

I dried my hands on a tea towel and turned out the kitchen light. I'd expected Libby to be engrossed in her favorite television show. Instead, she sat curled up in Jake's recliner, studying a shabby snapshot of two men and a boy leaning against the side of an old DeSoto.

My hand shook slightly as I drew it from her grasp. "Where did you find this?"

"Aunt M gave it to me. She said she didn't need it anymore and I could frame it if I liked."

I held the picture under the lamp to get a better look. Jake lounged on the right, his sailor hat pulled down almost to his eyes, one foot propped up on the running board, his elbow resting casually on his knee. Wesley stood in the middle, almost at attention, his uniform as impeccable as always. But the way he held his upper body—forward, as if poised for flight—gave away his impatience to be gone.

Billy stood to Wesley's left, one hand encased in a worn, leather baseball glove, the other clutching his favorite wooden bat. His Yankee cap was pulled down across his eyes in an obvious attempt to imitate Jake.

"It must have been hard, Mother." Libby's voice sounded pensive. "After I was born, I mean. With Uncle Billy dead and Daddy and Uncle Wes still off to war."

I started to answer, but Libby barely drew breath before she plunged on, and I could tell she'd been thinking about it for a while.

"It would be awful to stay alone while your husband's out at sea. Especially when you know he could get shot any minute and never come home again."

I nodded, but Libby didn't notice. She had retrieved the photograph and was studying it closely, her eyebrows drawn together in a frown. "I'm sure glad Daddy made it home all safe and sound. Nana Rose says Uncle Wesley was a casualty of war, but Aunt M told me he came home long enough to sign for a divorce, then went back to some bimbo on some godforsaken island in the Pacific."

"Liberty Jane!"

"She said it, not me."

I shook my head. It did sound just like Mary Margaret. "Well, you don't need to repeat it." I brushed back my daughter's silky hair and kissed her forehead. "You should get some sleep. Morning comes early, and you've had a busy day."

"Moth-er. I'm fourteen, not four." She unfolded herself and

waded through a sea of colored wrapping paper toward her room. "Daddy said to tell you he's in bed."

I started to put out the lights and follow, when she ran back and wrapped me in a hug.

"I hate guns and bombs and fighting," she whispered. "I sure hope there'll never be another war."